MORE VAMPIRE STORIES WITH BITE

Eternal

MORE VAMPIRE STORIES WITH BITE

EDITED BY

P. C. CAST

with Leah Wilson

BENBELLA

BenBella Books, Inc.
Dallas, TX

"Bloodshed" Copyright © 2010 by Amy Vincent
"Say Yes" Copyright © 2010 by Lilith Saintcrow
"Letters to Romeo" Copyright © 2010 by Nancy Holder
"The Other Side" Copyright © 2010 by Heather Brewer
"Drama Queen's Last Dance" Copyright © 2010 by Rachel Caine
"Thief" Copyright © 2010 by Jeri Smith-Ready
Introduction Copyright © 2010 by P.C. Cast

BenBella Books, Inc.
10300 N. Central Expressway, Suite 400
Dallas, TX 75231
www.benbellabooks.com
Send feedback to feedback@benbellabooks.com

Printed in the United States of America
10 9 8 7 6 5 4 3 2 1

Library of Congress Cataloging-in-Publication Data is available for this title.
ISBN 978-1-935618-01-0

Copyediting by Erica Lovett
Proofreading by Michael Fedison
Cover design by Sammy Yuen, Jr.
Text design and composition by PerfecType, Nashville, TN
Printed by Bang

Distributed by Perseus Distribution
www.perseusdistribution.com

To place orders through Perseus Distribution:
Tel: (800) 343-4499
Fax: (800) 351-5073
E-mail: orderentry@perseusbooks.com

Significant discounts for bulk sales are available. Please contact Glenn Yeffeth at glenn@benbellabooks.com or (214) 750-3628.

Contents

ETERNAL

Introduction

P. C. CAST

Oh boy, here I go, introducing *another* vampire anthology. How could I be involved with *another* group of vamp stories? I mean, they say readers are oversaturated, inundated, sick of, done with, and basically just all around bored with everything vampire. Come on, isn't it time vampires went back into their coffins?

Ugh.

Don't you hate it when "they" try to tell you what you should or shouldn't like? As I'm writing this introduction, I'm also outlining an essay due to release during the ALA's Banned Books Week. It keeps striking me as sublimely ironic that I'm preparing to write about enjoying freedom from censorship in one essay and in another I'm having to justify why a bunch of us are still reading what we want to read.

If you've bought this collection you either aren't sick of the "vampire craze," or you don't know what the hell

I'm talking about—you bought this 'cause the cover is cute and you thought this thing by P.C. Cast might be about the House of Night, so now you're confused and annoyed. If the latter is the case, sorry. This isn't a HoN story, but there are six other kick-ass stories collected here. So go on about your business, skip the rest of my intro, and happy reading.

For the rest of us I have several things to say about "the vam*pire!*" (please insert Andrew's voice from *Buffy*, season 7) and the hoopla about how "OMG, this whole vampire obsession is just insane; there are vampires/vampyres everywhere!" First, I don't think saying the market is oversaturated with vampire stories is very accurate. Can we please keep in mind that there are really only three things to write about: man vs. man, man vs. nature, and man vs. himself. (Three things. For all the books ever written. There's some oversaturation right there!) Saying there are too many vampire novels is like saying there are too many cars. Yeah, there may be quite a few rather large and sometimes gas-guzzling cars on the road right now, but what are they actually doing? It's simple. They're getting us from point A to point B, and that's something we always need. The type of vehicle, or genre, is only the wrapper. It's the ability to take us someplace that counts. Authors, readers, and critics need to stop stressing about fangs, garlic, blood lust, and pale skin and look under the hood for what matters: the writing. Did the story make you feel, wonder, hope? Did it leave you gasping, shaking, crying, laughing? Shouldn't that be what matters, and not the label under which the story's shelved?

And speaking of labels—they have always bothered me. When I taught high school I used to encourage teenage boys to read at least one good romance, something wonderful chosen from a bevy of talented authors like LaVyrle Spencer, Laura Kinsale, Diana Gabaldon, and Nora Roberts, to name just a few. Would it surprise you to know that every single young man who gave it a go, stepped outside his genre comfort zone, and read one of those books *loved it*? And subsequently read more and more. (I suspect they became better men for it, too—you are welcome, young ladies who married my ex-students.) So, really, I've been fighting the general annoyance of genres and the needless labeling they create for years. Can't we just not care where the darn book is shelved?

Anyway, I don't really get all the angst about oversaturation of the market and the oh-no-not-another-vampire-story attitude we're seeing bantered about on blogs that like to pretend to be "clever," "literary," and "snarky." Yawn. Right now I'm reading the latest in Kresley Cole's Immortals After Dark series. Uh, there are vampires in it. Again. There is also a great story carried by wonderful characters in unusual settings. Am I reading it because vampires happen to be a part of that? Nope. I'm reading it because Kresley knows how to tell a good story. Period.

And another thing: All of you readers who seriously heart vampires and are also aspiring authors, but are depressed and despondent because you really, *really* want to write a vampire story but have been told it's impossible to get one published because of "market oversaturation"? I say *thumb your noses at "them"*! Writing what you love is usually a very good idea. Go ahead and make your character a vampire if it rings your bell. That won't stop you from being published, not if that vampire character makes your reader feel, wonder, and hope and the story you're telling is compelling, your fantasy world vibrant, rich, and believable.

So, how does that happen? What makes us empathize with characters? What makes us laugh, cry, cringe, and worry with them? How are plots created that keep us up at night way past our bedtimes, and why do we sometimes feel like we're walking around all the next day in that special book world—whether that world is inhabited by vampires or not?

Well, sometimes it's as simple as setting a story during a compelling time of history, like Claudia Gray does in setting "Bloodshed" during WWII, where her characters grapple with trying to seek love and redemption, or in the case of Gray's heroine, Patrice, "maybe it was her own humanity she sought." Patrice's struggle made me care about her.

I also cared about Jack in Lili St. Crow's dark and disturbing "Say Yes." His perfection was absorbing and, vampire or not, I saw through the heroine's eyes and understood with her that "He was too real. Everything else was paper and plastic, and he was something else. It was like a hole in the world where something behind it was peeking through." Seriously— I would have said "yes" in less than a dead heartbeat.

Sometimes an author merges the familiar with her own unique vision and creates magic. That's what Nancy Holder does in "Letters to Romeo." Who doesn't want to revisit the tragedy of that love story and believe that our Romeo could—would—fight to live and then wait centuries for our return, the way this Romeo does for Juliet? In my heart I felt Romeo's "unrelenting loneliness. How did one still hope, after the first century, the second? What if he hadn't grabbed onto life and wrestled it from the catacombs? What if she had come back, and not found him waiting . . ." I want my Romeo, and I want him to wait for me for-friggin'-ever if he has to!

Then, after the bitter sweetness of star-crossed lovers and fortune's fool, Heather Brewer works her own heart-pounding version of the same familiar-but-not magic in "The Other Side," drawing us into Tarrah's horror as she teaches us about real monsters and madness:

> Terror painted her insides, but she forced herself to remain calm. Her hands slid along the pole, feeling, hoping that she'd be able to either yank or lift her way free, but her explorations found nothing but metal . . . that is, until they met with flesh. Someone else's flesh.

Yep, Ms. Brewer made me care, surprised me, and scared the bejeezus out of me.

I ached with Rachel Caine's Eve and Michael while they fought to discover the truth behind true love and loyalty in "Drama Queen's Last Dance." With them we find out "love is rarely that simple . . . or that painless." We know what Oliver means, not because he's a vampire but because Ms. Caine makes us *feel* it.

Finally, the brilliant Jeri Smith-Ready hits a homerun in "Thief" with Cass and Liam, and a relationship that transcends genre to get to the soul of all that is good and right in love, no matter the outside shell. Actually, Cass sums it up to Liam better than I when she finds out her fiancé is going to end up in a wheelchair:

> "You've always been the most beautiful boy I've ever known. You always will be. Okay?"
>
> His gaze slid off me, like he couldn't bear the truth in my eyes. "You mean on the inside, right?"
>
> "No!" I took his face in my hands and pressed my forehead to his. "You got any idea how late I lie awake at night, remembering every little inch of your face?" My fingertips traced his cheekbones. "I play back every kiss in my head in slow motion, again and again until I know I'll never forget it."

Curl up, all you vamp lovers, and prepare to experience *more than* a genre label. Prepare to enjoy a selection of good writing, fascinating characters, and excellent stories. But you're not surprised, are you? After all, you and I are in on the secret to a great read. We know it's more about heart than fangs, even if they do both deal with blood . . .

Bloodshed

A Story of Evernight

CLAUDIA GRAY

Boston, Massachusetts
September 1944

The air in the USO canteen was hazy with cigarette smoke, thick with longing. It would've been hard to say who was more easily enchanted by romance in this place. Maybe it was the young men going off to war, desperate for comfort and perhaps for someone to fight for. Or perhaps it was the young women, "junior hostesses" as the USO called them, who were supposed to drink and dance with them but never, ever to fall in love. Sometimes Patrice thought that rule only existed so that infatuations would also have the rich glamor of the forbidden; any kiss was sweeter in secret.

Patrice could have sneered at the naivety of the young people around her, if she wasn't the most bewitched of them all.

She glanced in the mirror for the fourth time that hour. Her reflection was slightly translucent, but any observer would probably think it was a trick of the smoke. These 1940s fashions suited her, Patrice thought: her white dress had navy piping and a matching belt that showed off her narrow waist. Bright red lipstick played up her smile, and her hair was curled up into a complicated twist. Appearance was important to her—always had been, always would be— but tonight she was even more particular than usual.

Once more, she glanced toward the door of the canteen—and just as the band swung into "The Nearness of You," Charlie walked in wearing his crisp army uniform. The smile that lit her up from within was soon matched by his own. They walked toward each other as though it were casual; the senior hostesses, middle-aged matrons who oversaw the USO canteen, would be shocked if Patrice did what she really wanted to do and ran immediately into his arms.

"There you are," she said as they took each other's hands. It was as much of a touch as they dared in public, and the warmth of his skin coursed through her like a pulse. "I've been looking for you."

"You know I got here as soon as I could." How she loved his deep, rumbling voice. "Nothing in this world could keep me away from you for long."

"Come on, then." Patrice put her fists on her hips, mock-angry. "You've kept me waiting to dance long enough."

By the time the band moved on to "Chattanooga Choo Choo," Charlie and Patrice had joined the crush on the dance floor. Girls with orchids in their Veronica Lake hair danced with soldiers, sailors, any man in uniform who could get into the USO canteen. Although there were still a few glances in Charlie and Patrice's direction, she was pleased to see that the novelty of black girls in the USO was apparently starting to fade. Black soldiers had always been able to come to the canteen—but at first, the USO hadn't seen fit to allow black girls in to dance with them. Dancing with white girls would probably have caused a race riot. So the black women of Boston had banded together and fought for the right to help entertain the soldiers before they shipped off to Europe or the South Pacific.

There weren't many other black couples on the dance floor—but Charlie and Patrice weren't alone, and to her astonishment, she thought they were almost accepted there. Which was the least the soldiers deserved, in her opinion; if black soldiers were good enough to fight and die for their country, then they ought to be good enough to share in the fun at the canteen.

That was why she had joined the USO herself—more out of pride in her right to do so than out of any concern for the war effort. Patrice had seen too many wars to get misty-eyed over this one.

But then, one night last month, Charlie Jackson had walked in, and for the first time in far too long, her cool heart had caught fire.

"Look at you," he whispered into her ear now as they swayed together to the tune of "String of Pearls." "The most beautiful girl in this room."

"Look at you." She couldn't keep the devilment out of her smile. "Dancing with the most beautiful girl in this room."

Charlie laughed so loud half the room stared at them.

Later, she drew him into one of the far corners of the room, supposedly to enjoy some Coca-Cola. (Patrice would've preferred something harder, but Charlie was a strict teetotaler.) Really it gave them a chance to sit close together, near enough that his knees brushed hers beneath the table.

Just as she began to open her mouth to say—something, anything silly and flirtatious, it hardly mattered what—he turned to her and solemnly folded one of her hands in both of his. The smile he'd worn all night had faded, and only now did she see how false it had been. Patrice knew what he was going to say before he said it, but that made it no easier to bear.

"We got word this afternoon. We'll ship out next week."

"Next week?" she whispered. "So soon?"

"You know they need every man over there."

"Just like I know I need you here."

"Patrice. Sweetheart." His voice cracked on the last word, and she could hear his plea to help him be strong. And for a moment, Patrice was ashamed of herself. This news scared her, but how much worse did it have to be for Charlie? Going over there to fight, perhaps to die—

She leaned closer to him and whispered in his ear, "Let's get out of here."

He went very still, as if he didn't believe what he knew she had to be suggesting. This was a moralistic age, one where unmarried men and women pretended they didn't go to bed together. But Patrice knew war had a way of breaking down such silly rules. "Are you sure?"

"Quite sure."

So she slipped out into the night with him and went straight to her apartment house for young women; the landlady, a patriotic sort, wasn't strict about the "no gentlemen visitors" rule if the gentleman in question wore a military uniform. Charlie came into her apartment, into her bed.

Patrice hadn't felt the warmth of a human body next to hers in so long. Too long. She had forgotten how the heat of a man's skin could sink into hers, through chest and belly and thighs. She had forgotten how his breathing changed, from even to quick to ragged and desperate. And how his heart would beat faster and harder until it thumped through his chest into hers, as if she could take his pulse and make it her own. She surrendered to him, and to her own hunger, in the moment that she saw Charlie was utterly lost in her. Then she could contain herself no longer. Clutching his shoulders, clinging tightly to him, she sank her fangs deep into his throat.

Blood. The weight of his body. The heat and taste of life. She swallowed deeply, metal and salt against her tongue, and for a moment the ecstasy was almost as good as being alive.

When Charlie collapsed unconscious onto her mattress, Patrice forced herself to stop drinking. She pulled back, panting, and licked her sticky lips. Charlie lay next to her, his breathing shallow but regular. The moonlight painted the muscles of his arms and chest, making him even more beautiful than he had been before.

She remembered what her sire, Julien, had told her almost a century before: the first bite is preparation. Charlie would awaken in a few hours, woozy and with his senses unnaturally sharpened, but he would almost certainly have no memory of what she had done. Only after that first bite—after the preparation—could she drink from him again, this time to the death, and have him rise again as a vampire, like her.

The decent thing to do would be to explain fully to Charlie what was going on, who and what she was, before she completed the change. Even Julien, cruel bully that he had been, had given her this courtesy. But Patrice wasn't sure decency was the same in wartime. She didn't have time for niceties, and she couldn't risk him rushing off, not understanding, and getting himself killed before she could make him see sense.

No Nazi was going to kill Charlie Jackson. Patrice intended to make him immortal before the Germans got the chance.

She shooed him back to base well before dawn, lest he be considered AWOL.

"I hate leaving you like this," Charlie whispered as he shrugged his shirt back on. He winced—how the noises and smells of the house must be tormenting him now, but he was too stoic to mention it. Probably he thought it no more than a headache. "It's not right, walking away from a lady after—well, after that. Not the way things ought to be done."

His modesty charmed her. Patrice snuggled deeper into her robe. "I'll see you this weekend. We'll have more time together before you go. And if you aren't on the base in the morning, they'll reprimand you, and you're too good to have something like that on your record."

Besides—you don't know it yet, but we're going to be together forever.

Charlie kissed her so deeply she almost forgot her resolve and took him back to bed—but then he straightened his cap and slipped out into the night.

Patrice sighed as she closed the door behind her. For a moment, she simply studied her surroundings, trying to measure the distances she'd traveled, the ways in which her world had changed and how it had remained the same. She had been born the daughter of a free woman of color in New Orleans and a plantation-owner father who paid the bills and would never, ever acknowledge his black child. Julien had freed her into an entirely different kind of existence. Unfortunately, he had also killed the first man she'd ever loved, Amos. For that, Patrice had doused Julien in lamp oil and set him ablaze. Her first kill: her sire, shrieking as he turned to charred dust.

She protected what she loved.

Since then, there had been men, but not love. Well—Ivan, perhaps—but no, she wasn't going to think about Ivan Derevko tonight. Charlie Jackson was the first guy to come along and make her feel as warm and sweet and overcome as Amos had. And the life Charlie led! He was a sergeant in the army. He'd even been studying at Howard University before the war broke out, and intended to become a professor of mathematics.

She'd grown up seeing black men in chains as slaves. To imagine him as a professor—

Could he do that, after I changed him?

But she pushed aside that momentary concern. Colleges didn't check to make sure students were alive, she figured. Even Evernight Academy didn't have a test to make sure its students were all dead. Charlie might look rather young for a while, but the addition of a pair of glasses could buy you several years; maybe he could be a professor for a decade or so before they had to move along to avoid attracting undue attention. That would be long enough, wouldn't it?

Patrice walked to her closet and pulled out the hatbox where she kept her most precious souvenirs. Within was a lace scarf she'd worn the last time she saw Amos, a fan that had belonged to her mother, a few bills of Confederate money, a bracelet from her first trip to Paris, some newspapers with headlines about the Crimean War, a Fabergé egg that held much more than sentimental value, a stole from a Moscow furrier, some Armistice Day poppies, and the older version of the Evernight Academy uniform.

She'd been considering returning to Evernight this fall— but now she had more interesting plans. Instead of teaching herself about the ever-changing world, she'd be teaching Charlie how to be a vampire.

Reverently she folded her pillowcase—the one with Charlie's bloodstains—and settled it in the hatbox before replacing the lid and pushing it back into the closet.

Charlie's next leave was on Sunday night, only two days before he was due to ship out to Europe. When he saw her, he flung his arms around her like he never wanted to let go.

"I can't stand the thought of leaving you," he whispered into her ear.

"Then don't think about it." *Because you won't be.*

Although they met at the canteen, neither of them was in any mood for dancing—Charlie because he was practically afire with worry for himself and for her, Patrice because she was impatient to get on with it. The canteen itself wasn't the same; half the girls had tearstained faces, and the boys were either shadowed with terror or wild with the cheap, feral glee some humans felt at the prospect of killing. With her experience of war, Patrice knew that the terrified were the smart ones. The band played upbeat songs, like "Don't Sit Under the Apple Tree," but the cheery tunes almost seemed to mock the darker mood in the room.

Within half an hour they'd walked out into the night. Patrice had assumed that Charlie would want to return to her room, though she figured she'd have to be the one to suggest it. But he led her along by the hand, walking with purpose to his steps, though they didn't seem to be headed anywhere in particular.

"You have to know what these past weeks have meant to me." His dark eyes could make her melt. "That I love you like I've never loved any other girl."

"And I love you." She couldn't add *like I've never loved any other boy*. To do that would be to betray Amos and the only love she'd ever known as a mortal woman. Being a vampire meant constantly negotiating between past, present, and future. Someday Charlie would understand this, too.

"A lot of the fellows—they're not bad men, but they just want a romance to comfort them before they go to war. What you and I have is more than that."

"I know, Charlie. It is for me, too." The moonlight outlined him in the night—his broad, muscular shoulders, his army hat, his masculine profile. With her night vision, Patrice could see that he hadn't knotted his tie as tightly as usual, that his collar was unbuttoned at the top. No doubt he didn't remember how he'd scratched his neck and why the skin there was slightly raw—those who were bitten almost never recalled the moment itself. But Patrice did. Remembering the warm velvet of his skin against her tongue and the rush of his blood filled her with longing.

He said, "I've never been one to run around with women. That's not how a Christian man should behave. I knew from the moment I met you that you were the kind of girl I'd been looking for all along. Sweet-natured. Beautiful. And sensible, too, not some flighty little thing."

"You're so sweet," Patrice said, but almost by rote, distracted as she was. She glanced around them: they were on the outskirts of a park, where the thick leaves of trees would shadow the streetlights and provide a bit of privacy. The time had come to kill and claim him.

Charlie was leading them toward the park already. He wanted them alone, too, though no doubt for different reasons. Patrice hid her little smile behind one hand.

"I don't have anything I can give you," he said. "Like—I mean, I don't have a ring."

No need to hide her smile anymore. "Oh, Charlie."

"But when I get home—and I promise I'm coming home for you, Patrice—when I get back from the war, I want us to be married. I know my family back in Baltimore will love you as much as I do."

In-laws. Perish the thought. "I want us to be together forever, too."

"And when this war is over, we can build a life together. The life I've always dreamed of." Charlie's grin shone; the fear of war had left him for a moment, as he looked toward a better future. "I don't know what Howard's policy is toward married students—never had to know, but I'll find out. And if we have to wait while we're engaged, that's all right, too, isn't it? I'll take double the courses. Get done even faster. Once I'm in graduate school, we can get married. Maybe buy a little house. Start our family."

"Our family," she repeated. The thought was all but alien to her, the shadow of a dream that had died for her almost before it began.

He hugged her close. His breath was warm against her ear. "I can't stop thinking about a bunch of little girls as pretty as their mama. Or a baby boy on your knee."

Patrice slowly put her arms around him in return.

"I'm going to love you all my life, Patrice. When we're old and gray, I know I'll feel the same way about you I do right now."

Old and gray.

He loved life as much as he loved her. Too much for her to rob him of it, no matter what. Letting him live the way he wanted meant letting him go—at least, for now. She had forgotten that love sometimes demanded sacrifice. Tears welled in her eyes.

Charlie felt her start to weep and cuddled her closer. "Honey, don't be scared. I know it's hard, but we'll be together again."

"When you're home from the war." And then she broke down in tears, surrendering him to the battle, and the dangers of mortal life.

Four Months Later

Evernight Academy admitted vampires of both sexes, but during wars, it practically turned into a girls' school. Battlefields were tempting, for vampires; even many women took part as nurses or other front-line support, if they could manage it. So many wounded, so many inevitable deaths—human blood ripe for the taking, and in most cases the killing was a mercy, guilt-free.

"That is one theory for the appeal of war to our kind," said Mrs. Bethany when Patrice mentioned it to her one day as a school assembly was about to begin. "My personal opinion is that men love war, and they are fools enough to run off to it whenever they can, even if they have had enough experience to know better."

"Not all men love war," said Patrice. Though she was only a few decades younger than Mrs. Bethany, she kept her voice respectful, her disagreement theoretical. Mrs. Bethany ruled over Evernight Academy as headmistress, and among vampires, hierarchy mattered. More than that—Mrs. Bethany had undeniable power. "I think most of them honestly believe it's their duty."

Mrs. Bethany raised an eyebrow. "Human men, perhaps, though I doubt even that. As for vampires—what loyalties can we owe to nations that will rise and fall a dozen times during our existences? Even those I would expect to know better fall prey to the lure of it." She held up a thin letter with the distinctive symbols of the navy on the envelope. "Another deferral for another semester. Yet Balthazar More is two centuries my senior, always entirely sensible in my experience, at least until now. He is of Puritan stock, one of the original settlers of the Massachusetts colony. Why should he feel a duty to fight the Japanese?"

They bombed us, Patrice wanted to say, but she knew better than to argue with Mrs. Bethany in one of her cynical moods. Besides, the rest of the students had gathered, and it was time to begin the assembly.

Mrs. Bethany's long skirt rustled as she ascended the podium in the great hall. "Girls, as you know, Evernight Academy must appear to the outside world to be a school like any other. Therefore it is appropriate for us to engage in war work, and this year we will again be leading a rubber drive in Riverton and other nearby communities. You will go from house to house and ask the residents for any old tires or other rubber items that can be spared. The school Studebaker will be made available to you for hauling the rubber to our collection point, and when we have gathered enough, we will donate it to the armed forces to be melted down for their use. I must remind all of you to be polite, to use your knowledge of the modern era to interact appropriately with the public, and to conduct yourselves as representatives of this school. Although I would once have thought it unnecessary to add this, last year's drive proved me wrong, so I will reiterate: it is *completely unacceptable* to kill humans in order to take their rubber goods. This is not in the spirit of the drive. Let's have none of it this time."

The assembly broke out into excited chatter—after a few months of relative isolation up in the Massachusetts hills, most of them were eager to get back out in the world and try their newfound knowledge about the way life was lived now. Patrice felt less of a charge than the others; with Charlie away at war, she hardly cared about being out and about. Better to stay here, to bury herself in schoolwork and try to forget the nagging question of what she was going to do when Charlie came home.

Then Mrs. Bethany's aide shouted out, "Mail call!"—and Patrice's name came first.

Smiling, she grabbed for the envelope, expecting another of Charlie's long letters from "Somewhere in Europe," as the soldiers always wrote to protect troop locations from becoming publicly known. He was a good correspondent, writing often, sharing funny stories about his fellow soldiers, his prayers for her well-being, his faith that this was a just and noble fight, and sometimes, when he had to, his reactions to the bloodshed he'd seen. When he did that, he always apologized for shocking her; she always wrote back that nothing he endured could shock her, because it was a part of him. She didn't add that she'd shed more blood than he could imagine.

But the letter wasn't from Charlie. It was from Charlie's mother.

"He's a prisoner of war." Patrice paced back and forth in Mrs. Bethany's carriage-house office. "Apparently he was captured in the Battle of the Bulge. Now he's at the Stalag VII-A camp in Bavaria, Germany."

Mrs. Bethany watched impassively. Probably she thought Patrice ridiculous, but Patrice didn't care.

"At first I was just glad he hadn't been killed," she continued, "but Mrs. Jackson says he's sick. You know as well as I do what war is. How captives are treated. And the Nazis think black men are lower than animals. Even the common people in Germany don't have the necessities of life anymore, so what are the chances Charlie will get the medicine he needs?"

"And what do you propose to do about this?" Mrs. Bethany steepled her hands over her desk.

Patrice hadn't really thought about it until that moment, but she knew instantly. The promise she'd made to herself months before returned more strongly, blotting out everything that had held her back before: no Nazi was going to kill Charlie Jackson.

"I'm taking a leave of absence from school."

"This can't be as simple as a mortal love," Mrs. Bethany said. Maybe she was so divorced from her old human life that she couldn't even understand how Patrice felt anymore. Though there was that silhouette on her desk—an image of a human man who must have died 150 years ago. "Do you think it's your duty to go to the battlefield, Miss Devereaux? Or do you, too, desire easy blood?"

Patrice imagined the Nazi soldier standing between her and Charlie, then imagined ripping that soldier open, draining him dry. "Both, Mrs. Bethany."

One corner of Mrs. Bethany's mouth lifted in a wry smile. "Then godspeed, Miss Devereaux."

Bavaria, Germany
Six Weeks Later

A harsh voice rang out, "*Hier, Kommandant!*"

Patrice huddled in a small gap at the base of an oak tree, cold with sweat. Flashlights swept through the forest, their beams scissored by the trunks of the trees that made up this vast forest. Although she was no more than a mile or two from Stalag VII-A, Patrice felt as though she might as well still have been halfway across the world from that POW camp, and from Charlie.

Getting here hadn't been easy. Pleasure travel to Europe simply didn't exist any longer, and even cargo shipping was rare, heavily guarded, and dangerous. Patrice had finally been able to stow away aboard a weapons shipment, and she'd spent the other time wondering whether German U-boat shells would count as "fire" and therefore have the power to kill her—to send her to the death beyond death. She suspected they would. Once arriving in France, she'd had to try to pass unnoticed in crowds, which was difficult in a nation with few black women.

But one of these women, a French nightclub singer and resistance worker named Josephine Baker, had proved both sympathetic and enormously helpful. With the fake papers she'd provided, Patrice had been able to get herself almost to the front. The rest had been running by night, hiding by day.

And the bloodshed she'd already seen had terrified her, not for herself but for poor Charlie.

He was such a gentle soul. Or at least he had been, before going to war. Although his letters had revealed some of the horrors he'd seen, Patrice knew now that Charlie had been editing them carefully. Because this was the greatest nightmare she had witnessed since the final years of the Civil War, worse even than the atrocities she'd seen during the Russian Revolution, and she suspected that even greater nightmares lurked deeper behind the front.

The thought of those nightmares being visited on her Charlie made Patrice want to run straight through the woods, without stopping, until he was again in her arms. But the Nazi patrol she'd just encountered had other ideas.

"*Ich glaube, das Mädchen ist hier versteckt!*" a soldier shouted. German wasn't one of the four languages Patrice spoke, but the voice was closer; that was enough to tell her it was a bad sign.

It's not as though they can kill me, she reminded herself. But the reassurance rang hollow. They didn't know what she was, but they could hurt her, perhaps even render her unconscious; at that point, they would think her dead. And if they buried her in consecrated ground, or—more likely— burned her corpse . . .

Don't think about it. Run.

Patrice dashed through the woods, ignoring the snap of twigs beneath her feet and the branches scratching gouges in her arms and legs. Her skirt caught on something but she simply tore it free and kept running. Machine-gun fire lit up the forest, strobe flashes and reports so loud they deafened her, but there was nothing to do but go faster. She could outrun any human alive.

But then one leg gave out from under her, and she fell.

She saw the wound before she felt it, a dark wet mess. The shock of the bullet's impact had temporarily numbed her to the pain, but when she put her hands to her left knee, she found not intact flesh and bone but a gory ruin. Patrice swore beneath her breath. The wound would heal given time, but with Nazi soldiers running toward her, guns in hand, time was something she didn't have.

Anger was sharper than any hunger. Patrice felt her fangs sliding into her mouth, and the killing rage came upon her. When the first soldier appeared in her line of vision, she leaped toward him—using her arms and good leg, jumping from all fours like an animal.

He went down under her, screaming when he saw the fangs for the first half-second before she savagely broke his neck.

Another soldier, and she tried to jump for him as well—but the pain from the gunshot finally blasted through her. Patrice collapsed to the ground, and it took all her strength not to cry out. They had her, they had her for sure—

And then another figure leaped from the woods and tore the Nazi pursuing her in two. The shadows split in front of her, and droplets of hot blood spattered on her cheek. Patrice lay utterly still in shock, except for the tip of her tongue, which shot out to capture the drops.

She watched, silently, as the new figure cut through the entire Nazi patrol. Even before his third kill, Patrice had recognized the style of fighting and the way he moved. But pain had made her giddy, and her recognition was only a very faraway fact, more amusing than anything else.

When at last the slim shadow came toward her, blood-soaked, she just watched him from her place on the ground until he said, in his thick Russian accent, "Patrice?"

"Ivan Derevko." She made a sound that was half cough, half laugh. "Fighting for Mother Russia again?"

"Always. God knows who you are fighting for, but I dare say you lost." Ivan stepped closer to her, so that she could see him more clearly in the moonlight. He wore a long gray woolen coat and a black scarf looped around his neck, both somewhat disheveled from the fight. His blond hair and beard were striped with blood, and his smile still showed his fangs; it was how she remembered him best.

"I have to get to Stalag VII-A. As fast as I can. You have to help me."

"I? I *have* to do nothing. Luckily for you, your charms are such that I will help you as soon as it would do any good. In other words, not yet."

Charlie was in a prison bunk, sick and maybe dying. "Damn you to hell."

"Our mutual sire took care of that for both of us. Convenient. But whoever it is you hope to kill, you won't be able to manage it until that leg has healed."

Patrice wanted to argue, but she wanted to sleep even more. That deep, powerful urge to rest was a sign that her vampire body was attempting to shut down and repair itself. "I don't trust you."

"Wise of you. And yet tonight, you have no other choice." Ivan stooped to lift her in his arms. His embrace filled her with memories of years gone by—or were those dreams? Patrice could no longer tell the difference.

She awoke in a house made of ivy.

No, Patrice realized—it was a regular house, but one so long-abandoned by humans that ivy had reclaimed the walls, the ceiling, even most of the floors. Ivy ignored winter and remained vividly green, its dark leaves defiant against the snow and ice that caked every other surface. The fireplace had been cleared out, or Ivan had simply started a fire there without caring if the ivy would eventually catch and burn down the entire structure. That would be like him.

Groggily she pushed herself up on her elbows. Ivan sat in the corner, on a metal chair that also was overgrown with ivy. His face remained as unearthly beautiful as ever: narrow but masculine, with high cheekbones and piercing blue eyes. Apparently Julien had turned him as a kind of work of art; at least, so Ivan claimed. But Patrice could believe it. He hugged his arms as though he were cold, and she realized that she was lying on his coat.

"I like what you've done with the place," she said.

"It's not much, but it's home." Ivan's wolfish grin made her smile despite herself. "Now, the story. For two weeks I've been tracking you. I recognized your scent—the style of your kills—but I told myself, Patrice is much too sensible to decide that wartime is the perfect opportunity to travel in Europe. I wasn't convinced it was you until I saw you for myself."

"The man I love is in a German POW camp. I'm here to get him out."

Ivan didn't immediately react, but Patrice could tell the smile was no longer entirely genuine. Then he surprised her—he laughed. "Still you are trying to replace me. Not so easily done."

"You replaced me well enough. Did I object when you took up with that Greek girl? What was her name—Athena?"

Ivan shrugged. "That was ten years after you left me. I shouldn't have expected you to object."

"Now it's twenty years after I left you. So let's put the past in the past." Patrice pushed herself the rest of the way up, so that she was sitting down instead of lying down. "You must hate the Nazis as much as I do. Won't you enjoy helping me? Think of the fun we'll have, killing them all."

"If I help you, it won't be for fun. And it won't be out of hate," he said quietly.

Rather than acknowledge the true meaning of his words, Patrice turned her attention to her knee. Dried blood was thick on her skin and her long woolen skirt, but the wounds had almost completely closed. Carefully she bent the knee; it still hurt too much for her to walk easily, but it was much better. Her vampire healing would restore her fully by sundown.

"Once it turns dark, I'm going, Ivan. Are you with me or not?"

"I'm with you. Always. You know this, of course." Ivan sighed and leaned his ivy-covered chair back; vines went taut and snapped. "So, tell me about this man who so enchants you. Human, I assume; no self-respecting vampire would remain in a POW camp for very long."

"Human. Charlie Jackson. Studying mathematics at Howard University."

"When and how did he learn what you really are?"

Patrice could no longer meet Ivan's eyes. "You've heard all the details I intend to tell you."

He laughed so loudly that Patrice tried to shush him, but he wouldn't be silenced. "You haven't told him! This Charlie thinks you're a sweet young girl from home. What will he think when you appear before him as the avenging monster you really are?"

"Charlie loves me." Her voice sounded overly sharp, even to her, but she wouldn't be mocked by Ivan—not about this. "And I love him. He's a good man who's sick and suffering in a camp run by people who think he's even less than an animal. I'm going to save him. Nothing else matters."

Ivan's smile had softened. This, too, reminded her of other days. "When I met you, I believed you cared about nothing but clothes and champagne and fun. Fun for me, too, I thought. But I did not fall in love with you until I learned how fierce you are."

Briefly Patrice remembered a long-ago sleigh ride in the snow, furs heaped around her to ward off the bitter chill of the Russian winter. She and Ivan had been running for their lives, and she had felt no fear, only the savage joy of the hunt. With Charlie, she had shared so much laughter and warmth, but never a moment like that.

But this could change.

Ivan continued, "War brings this savagery out in humans. In your Charlie, too. He's not the man you once knew. He has been to war. He knows what it is to kill. Be ready for that."

Patrice tried not to listen. She closed her eyes and thought instead of dancing with Charlie in the USO canteen. Although she could bring every other detail to mind—the smell of cigarette smoke, the crispness of Charlie's uniform, the laughter of the other junior hostesses on the dance floor—she couldn't quite recall any of the music. The only sound was the crackling of the fire.

Three hours after sunset, Patrice and Ivan huddled together at the edge of a grove of trees. The cold, hard ground that stretched out before them had been roughly cleared, and it was mostly a mess of frozen mud between them and the barbed-wire fences of Stalag VII-A. Searchlights periodically swept the perimeter, but by now she knew their pattern. Even with her knee still stiff, Patrice could move faster than any human. And if the barbed wire ripped her flesh as she climbed over, well, that would heal, too.

"There are occultists among the Nazis," Ivan murmured. His breath was cool against her ear; vampire's breath never fogged in the winter. "I should imagine no more than a few dozen of them in the entire Third Reich have any idea what they would truly be dealing with, if presented with a vampire. But if one of them is here tonight, it will go badly for us."

"Badly for me," she said. "You're staying out here."

"I thought you said you wanted my help."

"I do. If I get hung up inside the POW camp, I'll need someone to come in after me and Charlie. And if we're pur-

sued afterward, you could cover us. But while I'm trying to
sneak around in there? One more person is just double the
noise."

"I hate it when you prove that you're smarter than I am."

"You know I can't help it."

They gave each other the mocking look that always used
to make them laugh, but the humor was darker now.

Ivan said, "Have you any idea how to find him?"

"I know he's in the infirmary, so it will just be a matter of
finding the sign."

"How did you discover this?"

"His mother wrote it in her last letter."

"You're writing to his mother! *Bozhe moi*, when you play-
act at being human, you don't stop halfway, do you?"

Scowling, Patrice said, "Do you want to keep making
sarcastic comments, or shall we begin?"

Ivan stepped slightly back among the trees, silently indi-
cating his acceptance of her plan. Turning her attention back
toward the camp, Patrice waited for the searchlight to slide
slowly past one more time—and then she ran.

Full vampire speed: she rarely used it, rarely had the
need. But now she felt the joy of pushing her body beyond
its old mortal constraints. Although her knee burned in pro-
test, it was pain Patrice could easily bear. So were the stabs of
barbed wire in her palms, against her knees. Her skirt ripped
as she vaulted over the fence, but that didn't matter. Nothing
mattered except finding Charlie.

Patrice scrambled across the camp yard; if she understood the rotation of the guards, nobody would walk directly

past her for a few minutes yet. Each barrack was neatly labeled, and hopefully the infirmary would be, too.

There! *Krankenstation*—that was the German word for it. No lights, no guard at the door; these prisoners weren't held captive by bolts or locks but by that barbed-wire fence around them.

For a moment, Patrice couldn't think about the danger they were in or the difficult explanations that lay ahead. All she could think about was that she was within moments of seeing Charlie again. How stupid of her to be happy—to be like a human girl about this—but there was no denying it.

Silently she stepped inside. Though the infirmary bunks were full, no doctor or nurse was on duty. These men were expected to heal or die on their own, at least at this hour of the night.

Immediately Patrice saw him—Charlie was the biggest man there. Though he was so much thinner than before—

She crept to his bedside, tears welling in her eyes. "Charlie?" she whispered. "Charlie, wake up."

He opened his eyes. He didn't show any surprise, only a slow kind of wonder. "Patrice."

"I've come to take you home."

"I—always knew—" His breath came shallow and fast, like his lungs couldn't take in air anymore. He was even sicker than she'd feared: pneumonia, or perhaps even tuberculosis. "Always knew—you weren't just a girl."

The shock felt like falling into the coldest snow, but she knew better than to overreact. "What do you mean, Charlie?"

"Knew you were—an angel."

"An angel come to take you home. Put your arms around my neck."

Charlie tried to do so, no doubt believing that this was merely a dream, or some kind of vision before death. Though his grasp was weak, it would do. Patrice called upon her vampire strength and lifted him from his sickbed. Though he was six inches taller than her and probably seventy pounds of muscle heavier, she could manage it easily. Getting him over the fence—harder, but still within her power. As she settled him in her arms, his rough black blanket fell to the floor. She considered trying to grab it but discarded the idea. No doubt the cold would be bad for him, but maybe that wouldn't matter for much longer.

She walked out of the infirmary, leaving the door open behind her; let them believe Charlie had escaped. Almost as soon as she walked into the yard, though, she heard a guard call out, "*Haltestelle!*"

And then she could only run for the fence, knee stinging, Charlie strangely light in her arms. A searchlight panned toward her, almost blinding her with its sudden blaze, but she had senses beyond sight.

"What's . . . what's happening . . ." Charlie rasped.

Patrice couldn't answer. She hoisted him to one side to get one hand free and vaulted for the fence. Barbed wire sank into her palm, tore at her knees, but she was moving almost too quick to feel it. Machine-gun fire rang out, but missed her.

She and Charlie slammed hard into the frozen ground as they fell outside the stalag fence, but Patrice didn't even slow down, just swung him back into her arms as she continued running. Footsteps and shouts echoed behind her, but she never glanced back.

As she crashed into the grove of trees, she had to slow down, and she heard her pursuers gaining on them. Then she heard their screams, and Ivan's laughter.

Yes, it was always good to have backup.

As she sank to her knees and settled Charlie upon the earth, Patrice sucked in a deep breath to soothe herself, and smelled blood.

The machine-gun fire hadn't missed after all. Charlie was badly hit.

Patrice put one hand on his chest, which was wet and hot with blood. He was all but unconscious now, quivering in what were likely to be his death throes.

And she realized she felt—relief.

There was no choice to make now, no compromise. It didn't matter how much Charlie loved life; it didn't matter whether he would have chosen to become a vampire or not. He was dying. The only chance he had now was to change, and to join Patrice in immortality.

She briefly remembered the conversation she'd had with Mrs. Bethany at Evernight. This, Patrice knew, was the real glory of war for vampires. In a time of bloodshed, there were so many opportunities to kill without guilt.

For humans, too, she supposed. But they didn't matter now.

Patrice leaned over Charlie and gave him a quick kiss. "Don't be afraid," she whispered, in case he could still hear. "I'm going to make it all better."

As her fangs slid into her mouth, she thought for an instant of what it had been like to dance in Charlie's arms at the USO canteen—to lean against his chest and hear his heart beat.

Then she bit into his throat again, knowing him prepared for the change, and silenced that heartbeat forever.

"I'm still hungry," Ivan complained. "But you won't think of me any longer, will you?"

"You hush. You've eaten plenty. Remember how it is when you first wake up?" Patrice had not left Charlie's side throughout that night. A few more Nazi patrols had come out searching for their lost comrades, which was why Ivan really had no business complaining about hunger pangs. And while she was grateful for his help, she wished he would have the decency to leave them alone for a few minutes.

Morning was dawning. Soon Charlie would rise.

He lay, still and dead, in the center of the ivy cottage. The ivy's life despite the winter's cold seemed to echo Charlie's coming resurrection. Although the air was bitterly cold, they didn't dare build another fire. Smoke against the gray morning sky would reveal their location, if any soldiers were fool enough to still be searching for them.

"He looks like your long-lost Amos," Ivan said lazily. "How predictable of you."

Charlie did bear a strong resemblance to Amos, but it wasn't so unremarkable to prefer a certain "type," was it? "I love him for himself."

"You love him for the illusion he represents. I look forward with great interest to seeing the two of you confront each other's reality."

Enough of his nonsense. "Don't you want to check the edge of the forest again? There could still be soldiers out there. If you're so hungry."

"You think Charlie will awaken and you will share a rapturous reunion. And if it is like this, I will accept your suggestion and gratefully miss the romantic scenes that will take place. But it's not always so easy, is it?"

"It was for me."

"And for me. But not for all."

Patrice was about to tell Ivan to stop his Russian doomsaying for once, but that was the moment when Charlie's foot twitched.

Both she and Ivan went very still, and he took a couple of steps backward. While he might mock her newest love affair, Patrice knew that Ivan understood the importance of this moment.

Slowly, so slowly, Charlie's eyes opened. He remained very still, as though he did not trust the new sensations and powers flowing through his undead body. When he glanced at Patrice, she smiled at him gently, but made no sudden moves. If he remembered his death clearly, he might at first feel some illogical fear of her. She wanted him to understand that he was safer than he'd ever been. Nothing could hurt him now.

Then his gaze flicked toward the corner, where the last of the Nazi soldiers who had pursued them slumped against the wall. The soldier was unconscious but alive. Charlie's expression hardened, and he worked his jaw, no doubt feeling the first emergence of his fangs.

"Are you hungry?" she whispered. "Then drink."

Charlie vaulted from the floor so fast Patrice could hardly see him, ripping at his first victim so savagely that blood spattered wastefully on the falls. He hunched over the body, more monster than man, and there was nothing of Charlie in him. Nothing at all.

Don't be stupid, she told herself. *He just rose. There's nothing like that first hunger.* But next to her she could sense Ivan becoming wary.

When Charlie had sucked all the blood he could from the corpse, he threw it against the wall so hard that bones crunched. He turned back to them, his face a mask of anger. "More."

"Good hunting awaits you," Ivan said, calm and pleasant. Patrice felt a surge of gratitude. "We can go into the forest now, look for foxes and deer. And tonight, we can revisit your German captors, if you would like. They would not like, I assure you."

"Now," Charlie growled.

"Get a hold of yourself." The sharpness in her voice shocked her. "You're still you, Charlie. Just a vampire now."

The word vampire seemed to snap some sense back into him. Charlie rose from his crouch, his bloodied prison clothes hanging from him in rags. "I remember . . . I remember you bit me."

"That's right. I bit you. I changed you, so you wouldn't die."

"You're a vampire, too," he said. Charlie didn't sound shocked or horrified. More . . . angry. "You always were?"

"For almost one hundred years." Patrice glanced briefly at Ivan. "The two of us, Ivan and I—we were changed by the same vampire. That means we can always find each other. Just like you'll always be able to find me, because I'm your sire."

Charlie frowned. "Sire?"

"There's a lot to understand. We'll explain everything, and we'll get you all the blood you need. It's easy in wartime."

"You lied to me," Charlie said.

Patrice winced, but she was not one to back down easily. "Soon you'll be lying, too, and you'll understand why it's necessary."

He was starting to smile—a smile she didn't like. Ivan took a step closer to her. But now Charlie was laughing. "It's all been a lie. Everything they ever taught us in school or in church. Nothing but lies."

"Stay calm. You need to remember who you were, to decide what you want to be," Patrice said, but he didn't seem to care.

"Monsters are real!" Charlie shouted with glee. "You can rise from the dead without any help from Jesus. You can live by killing other people, and nothing's ever going to punish you. What's hell? We never have to worry about it, do we?"

"You can make a hell of earth easily enough," Ivan said. "I don't advise it."

"All my life, I studied and worked. Never took a drink. Never took a girl to bed until I thought it might be my last chance before I died, and even then I meant to marry her." *Her*, Charlie said, as though Patrice weren't there in the room. "And it was for nothing! Life begins after death—the preachers didn't lie about that. But heaven can't be as sweet as drinking that Nazi's blood."

"Charlie!" Patrice cried. But he was lost in a wild, thrilled delight that didn't include her. Not yet, anyway—when he calmed down he'd probably be more interested in company. But already she knew that Ivan had been right. She'd loved an illusion, and the memory of Amos; she'd never really known Charlie at all. Nor had he known her. They had just been two more enchanted lovers at the canteen, mesmerized by war and the romance of the forbidden.

"I'm going hunting," Charlie said. He didn't ask for a teacher, and why should he? She knew his instincts would guide him. "Don't try to stop me. Nothing is ever going to stop me again."

He ran for the door. For one last instant he was silhouetted against the pale dawn sky—then Charlie was gone. All of him: body, soul, life, love, illusion. There was nothing left for her.

"If he doesn't recklessly get himself slain in the next few days, someday Charlie will come looking for you," Ivan said. "He'll be able to find you. I cannot yet tell whether he'll come out of love or hate. Or perhaps merely desire. You do have this effect on men."

"I'll deal with it when it happens." Patrice couldn't look Ivan in the face. "So. You were right. Don't pretend you're not happy about it."

"As with many things, the possibility was more enjoyable than the reality. Do you think I enjoy seeing you hurt?"

And that—the knowledge that he could see her pain, that her beauty and her coolness had been inadequate to hide that wound—was what brought Patrice to tears. She could bear anything—even death, even loss—but she could not endure being exposed before anyone.

Patrice crumpled against the wall, hands covering her face so Ivan couldn't see any more. But the sobs wouldn't stop coming. At least he knew her well enough not to try to hold her.

"Patrice. Don't do this to yourself," he murmured as she wept. "You're too strong to mourn the loss of a mere dream."

Did Ivan never have any dreams of his own? What had Julien taken from him, when he changed Ivan into a vampire? Patrice didn't know. Didn't want to know. She'd wanted to be out dancing again, with her hair done just so and a pretty dress on, ready to dance and flirt and play the part of the silly young girl she'd never been. The haze of the cigarette smoke in the USO canteen had helped to hide her true nature—even from herself—for a time.

Ivan said, "If I could understand one thing, I would want to understand why you only love the ones you can't keep."

"Stop it," she sobbed. "Just stop it. If you can't give me something better to think about, then don't say anything. Or go. Maybe you should go."

Ivan didn't go. He stood there, a slender shadow in a long gray coat, pale against the faded ivy leaves that covered the wall.

Maybe it was Amos she had been chasing, the shade of the man she'd lost too soon, too long ago. Or maybe it was her own humanity she'd sought. Either way, what a fool she'd been.

Although it took her many more minutes to collect herself and stop crying, Ivan said nothing else until Patrice had dried her eyes. As she straightened up, still disheveled but at least something like herself again, Ivan finally took a step toward her.

"You were in Paris," he said. "Since the liberation."

She'd told him this while they'd waited for her knee to heal. "Yes."

"I haven't been there since the 1920s. Is it still beautiful?"

"The war has left its mark," Patrice replied. "But of course it's still beautiful. It's *Paris*."

"Then I think I should like to see Paris again. And I think the journey there, while hazardous, could be quite delightful in the right company." How clever Ivan was. How wise. He knew the best thing to do was to pretend her breakdown had never happened. "Will you accompany me, Patrice? When we get to Paris, we'll drink champagne and stay up all night and create no end of scandals. And we'll kill every Nazi we see on the way there."

Patrice straightened herself, smoothed her hair, and took Ivan's arm. Somehow she managed to smile. "You always did know how to show a girl a good time."

Say Yes

LILI ST. CROW

That Friday the party was up in the hills, some ratfaced kid's parents were gone and a whole fake adobe mansion thrown open, throbbing with rave music. As soon as we got there I snagged us a couple of beers from a passing boy with a cooler full of ice and brown glass bottles, and Chelsea and I cased the place.

The hardcores were doing coke in one of the designer bedrooms upstairs. The banister had already been slid down. The punch bowl had probably already been spiked, and when we found the quietest back bedroom there was already a couple sprawled out across the water bed. The guy was a lacrosse star at St. Ignatius, and the girl was from one of the public schools. Nobody we knew. She looked glaze-eyed, her tangled brown hair spread out in a mat, eyeliner dripping down her cheeks. The lacrosse star's naked ass had pimples.

We left them alone and went back downstairs. The huge circular living room had a fireplace and a mass of kids hopping around to the half-assed DJ's attempt at trip-hop coolness. Girls in worn-thin designer jeans and cropped shirts that showed their bellies, jewelry winking. Boys in prep or jock costumes, some in loosened St. Ignatius uniforms. There was a sprinkling of Marys—girls from St. Mary of the Sacred Heart, Ignatius' sister school, instantly recognizable in the blue and green plaid skirts Chel and I also wore, the almost-knee-high socks, the Mary Janes and whatever shirts we threw on at the end of the school day. Some of them still had the Peter Pan collared white button-ups on, but they'd unbuttoned them down and camis peeked out through the top. You could always tell a Mary by the long hair, the healthy scrubbed skin, the clear nail polish, and the neutral lip gloss.

We don't all look alike, but it's close.

Chelsea took a long swig off her beer and rolled her blue eyes. I shrugged. It was as close as she would get to admitting I was right and this was a complete waste of time. We should have gone to the Rose. Yeah, it's an all-ages club and it sucks, but it was better than this.

The music was a loss, so we headed into the kitchen. Big beefy frat-boy types were doing shots off the counter. One of them staggered and put his head down like a bull, the blue fug of cigarette smoke wreathing his head. He looked just about to vomit, so we got an armful of cold beer bottles and retreated.

The patio was almost a complete loss, too. Someone had already been tossed into the pool and was shrieking, and there were two kids throwing up in the manicured bushes. Someone passed Chel a joint, she took a drag. There was a forgotten corner to the patio, two deck chairs sitting lonely under madrone trees. The stars were out, clear and cold though the night was warm, and the first breath of the Santa Anas was flirting with the sides of the canyons and the valley. It smelled like hot dust and chlorine from the pool. The music was too loud to be a comforting heartbeat, but it was close.

"Don't say it." She handed me another beer.

I shrugged again. My keychain had a dainty silver bottle opener, so I cracked both mine and hers.

"We can always leave." Her throat moved as she took a long hit off the bottle and passed me the joint. Even when she was drinking you could see the ballet classes every Mary has to take, classified under "deportment" and graded. It's so fifties, but it's what our parents pay for. "Go to the Rose."

The smoke stung my lungs. I held it for a long time. "It'll be the same there without the beer," I finally said. We clicked bottlenecks and sat back on the deck chairs, legs stretched out, ankles crossed and skirts safely tucked. I watched over the polished tips of my Mary Janes as one of the kids throwing up in the bushes staggered toward the kitchen door. "Jesus."

"I hope this kid knows a good cleaning service." She laughed, and the music started a screeching feedback loop. "God*damn*. Annoying."

I took a long draft. It slid cold down my throat. I hate the taste of beer, it's yeast in a bottle. But it was chilly and would give me a buzz. "Did Jenny get her results yet?"

"Not yet. And no period." Chel sucked in her cheeks. "Poor kid."

"Well, everyone knows how Marty is." I shifted uncomfortably on the deck chair. Thank God Chel had told me about him in time. When I'd moved here, I'd thought he really liked me.

That's the way he is with everything female, though. At least, everything female he thinks he can get his meat into. But he's a popular Iggie. His dad's in plastics or something. Bought his Junior a red convertible. It was like every cliché about midlife crisis come to life and projected onto a hapless kid.

"And she *was* voted Most Likely To Graduate Knocked-Up, If At All. In our highly unscientific personal poll." Chel giggled and so did I. It was nasty, but satisfying. Like nachos. We finished off the joint in companionable gossip, and the familiar soothing blanket of warmth spread all through me.

That was when she saw him. "Oh, wow. Hold *everything*."

I looked up, across the frothing mass of the pool. More kids had jumped in, clothes and all. And someone, of course, had poured dish soap or something in it, so great opalescent banks of bubbles crawled toward the molded-concrete rim.

It was just like every other party this year.

Except for him.

He stood by the French doors to the dining room, flung wide open to let in the night. He wasn't tall or even very cute. Here you've got to be blonde, snub-nosed, long-legged cheerleader material. Like Chel.

He had dark curly hair like me, more actual curls than my just-waves. Dark eyes and perfect olive skin. Normal face, nice and regular, nothing out of the ordinary.

But there was something about him. He stood there like he had all the time in the world, his sneakers placed carefully and his shoulders relaxed, hands in his pockets. A simple white button-down and jeans, his hair mussed and a thin gold necklace with a small white pendant nestled just below the hollow of his throat.

He was looking right at us.

Chel drew in a short, sharp little breath. I knew that sound. The cat had just found her next mouse.

I looked away quickly, studying the soap foam. Where was it all coming from? The kids weren't thrashing around enough for all of it.

Jets, I decided. Or whatever they'd put in the pool to make the bubbles.

"He's looking right over here." Chel had a good *sotto voce*, her lips barely moved even when she had to be heard over the thumping music.

We had lots of practice in class. St. Mary's is strict. But there are ways of getting around it, especially if the teachers think you're a brain. It's hard treading that line between smart and popular. You have to choose one or the other. Chel had the pop covered, I settled for doing all our homework and tagging along.

The sheen on the wall of bubbles looked sick. Like a slug-trail. I took another long draft of beer. My stomach was sour.

So was the rest of me. The feedback was beginning to give me a headache. Thank God it cut off just then, replaced by another pounding beat. Even the windows were flexing. It was a question for the ages: could the Eternal Dude make a sound system so loud even His eternal windows would shatter?

Betcha they wouldn't cover that in Theology class.

"Oh God, do I look okay?" Chel wanted to know.

"You look fine." Just like usual. She looked like a California dreamboat. And it poured off her in waves, hot interest. I could tell we were going to be replaying this all night. We'd probably go for late-late fries and milkshakes at Druby's and then to her house, where I was technically supposed to be staying the night. We'd get in about 3 or 4 A.M., get ready for bed, and then lay in her room giggling and talking about this very moment until she fell asleep. Because if I fell asleep she would poke me. "You look hot."

"I should've changed."

We hadn't changed because she'd been all in a hurry to hang at the mall and then zoom to the party. As a result we were part of the unbuttoned-dress-shirt-and-camisole crowd. "Schoolgirl is hot this year," I muttered.

"Schoolgirl's always hot." She shifted a little bit. I could tell she was raising her chin, because her mother was always on her about it. *It takes years off your age in photographs, sweetheart. Stand up straight.*

He must've been getting closer. The bubbles climbed up. In two years I'd be graduated, I'd go to whatever college would have me, and Spring Break would happen in Cancun or something. There would be shit like this all the time.

I hunched my shoulders. Took the last long six-swallow burst of beer, and was faced with the decision to belch like a linebacker now or in five seconds when the guy got to us. I chose now and stifled it with a ladylike hand. Chelsea about had a fit, trying to laugh with her chin up and her posture okay while lounging in a deck chair with kiped beers.

"Hi." He didn't quite have to shout to make himself heard over the music. Nice voice.

"Hi!" Chelsea chirped. "Want a beer?"

"Sure." He wasn't averse to the notion. Of course, who would be at a party like this?

There was an awkward silence. Both of them were looking at me. I gave Chelsea a sideways glance and cracked one of the beers, handed it up to him. I had to stretch and sit up to do it, and I kept my fingers on the bottom of the bottle so I didn't touch him. I went back to studying the pool.

He noticed I wasn't looking. "Did I interrupt something?"

"No, no, it's cool. She's just tragic. I'm Chelsea."

Tragic. That was a good word for it. I squeezed my knees together and leaned back in the chair. Maybe another beer was the answer.

"Jack. You go to St. Mary's."

Well, he got no points for stating the obvious. There was a beat or two of silence. If I was interested at all, now would be the time for me to be polite and introduce myself.

I didn't. It would only be grief. I knew the rule—if she was interested, I didn't even get to look. I was the accessory girl here, the brain to her looks. It was my job to be snarky and supportive.

Small price to pay for basking in her borrowed glow. Or at least, it seemed that way when we became "best friends."

I've been on the unpopular end of the stick. I don't want to revisit it.

Chel laughed brightly and stepped into the spotlight. "Yeah, you got us. Do you go to Ignatius? You look familiar."

What a lie. He didn't look familiar. He looked as far away from familiar as it was possible to get.

"No, I'm public. They think it's good for me."

"Shit, I'm sorry."

They both laughed. The flirtation settled into its normal course—Chel bright and sunny, the guy acting cool, and me on the sidelines watching.

What the hell. I cracked another beer.

We didn't have to wait for the bathroom, thank God, and we locked ourselves in. "How am I supposed to get home?" I folded my arms as she plunked herself down to pee. Whoever decorated this place was into peach-scented candles and little peach-shaped soaps. It was disturbing.

She actually flipped her hair at me while sitting on the pot. "God, don't be such an asshole. Bebe's here, she can drive you. Or Alicia. Come on. He's cute."

"You're ditching me." I barely glanced in the mirror. My hair was still a mess. No amount of product would make it behave. Goddammit. "For a boy who goes to *public*, for Chrissake."

"He's hot. Call a cab. Jesus."

"Slut."

"Jealous bitch."

I let out a gusty sigh. "Can I have your keys at least, get my bag out of your trunk? And do you have a fucking condom?"

"*All* condoms are *fucking* condoms, it's what they're *for*." The old joke broke us both up. I was pretty buzzed. So was she. None of it was important anyway. "I'm not going to screw him. Jesus. He's just really hot. I like him."

"You should be careful." It was wrong, or at least it felt wrong. We went on the buddy system. She could use me as an excuse to get away from a guy who got too grabby.

"Thanks, *Mom*." She finished and wiped. "Look, it's just—"

"It's fine. I'll get home somehow." I waited for my turn to pee.

She wouldn't look at me. Her cheeks were pink and her eyes were bright. Was she sweating? Just a little? "My door's unlocked, just pop the trunk."

I shrugged again. "I'll lock it after I do."

"You're such a worrywart. Jesus. Who's going to steal it with a bunch of rich kids around?"

Rich kids are the worst kind of thieves. Going to private schools had opened my eyes to that, at least. I didn't say it. She wouldn't understand. "Fine. Move. Let me pee."

That cracked us both up pretty good. We were friends again by the time we opened the bathroom door and she hurried off down the hall, waving over her shoulder at me. Her hair moved in a golden wave, her long legs smooth and unblemished; she switched her hips before she got to the stairs and disappeared. A redheaded girl in a strappy satin dress, exactly the wrong color blue for her skin tone, pushed past me into the bathroom.

I tucked a tiny peach-shaped soap in my skirt pocket. I'm a rich kid, too.

That was the last time I saw Chelsea alive.

I was hungover and my feet hurt from dancing. Bebe and the gang decided the party was tragic as soon as I hooked up with them. They headed to the Rose, so I went, too, after I retrieved my bookbag from Chel's little red convertible. I'd closed it up nice and tight.

But when your dad comes in your room without knocking and says, "What did you do?" with his eyes narrowed and his lips drawn tight, none of that matters.

"I didn't do anything." I peered up at him. My mouth was sour and my head hurt. Morning sunlight fell in through the curtains I'd forgotten to pull closed.

"Five minutes and I want to see you downstairs." He gave me the patented Legal Eagle Stare, the one that makes people sweat when they're giving testimony.

I wondered just how drunk I'd gotten last night. It wasn't horrific or anything. I'd just been on a steady buzz all night, and did a couple of shots before Bebe dropped me off. She almost took out our mailbox on the way out of the driveway, too. But no harm done.

When I got downstairs, still almost-retching over the taste of toothpaste and my face stinging from cold water, my heart was beating like thunder. The fat guy in the breakfast nook all but shouted *cop!* Our housekeeper, Consuela, had disappeared. And Dad's hazel eyes were still narrowed.

I edged into the room and that's when the questioning started. I figured out pretty early it was Chelsea they were after, not me—and when the cop started in on me about Jack I got a bad feeling. A *really* bad feeling. Adults just don't ask these kinds of questions unless something's happened.

I surprised myself by starting to cry.

"That's enough," Dad said. And for once I was glad he's a total asshole. I mean, he can't help it. He's a lawyer.

"Can she come downtown and give a statement?" The fat man looked like he didn't think Dad was going to go for that, and his halitosis was making my nonexistent breakfast roll around inside my stomach. "And help come up with a sketch of this Jack kid? You—" This he directed at me. "You don't have any idea where he goes to school or any-thing, right?"

"He said he was public." I was actually hugging myself, the sharp points of my elbows digging into my cupped palms. "Going to public school," I added when the cop looked blank.

"Of course she'll cooperate." Dad stood up, smoothly, and the cop stood up, too. Morning sunlight poured in through the kitchen windows and scraped the inside of my brain clean. It was a Saturday morning before noon and something horrible had happened.

"Wait." I unhugged myself long enough to grab the back of a chair. "What happened? You still haven't told me what happened."

The cop gave me a long, weird look. He had piggy little eyes, and his gaze dropped below my chin and ended up on my chest. I was in the cami I wore last night, no bra, but still, a cop shouldn't look like that.

"We don't know," he said finally. "She's just missing."

Right then I knew he was lying. But they lie all the time, all of them. It's no big deal. Except right now it was, because it was Chelsea.

Dad got rid of him and came back into the kitchen. "Is there anything you didn't tell him?" He had his lawyer voice on. Whenever he argued with Mom he used that voice. I think it's why she left him. But he got custody, because of the prenup guarding his money and because he's an attorney.

I didn't know why he even went for custody instead of dumping me on Mom. He barely ever talked to me. But he's a collector. I guess I was just one more thing to keep when Mom committed the sin of leaving.

"Like what?" I held onto the chair. My knuckles were white. "She said she was going with him. I went with Bebe. What's really going on?"

He gave me the same weird look. But he didn't look mad, for once. "Get ready to go. We're going to be spending an hour or two in the police station."

They found her naked in a ditch outside of town with her throat shredded and her legs obscenely splayed. I know because I saw it on the news when I got home, before the sketch of Jack's face went up. The sketch artist hadn't gotten him right, mostly because I couldn't put it into words. How he was *different*. I couldn't even explain it to myself.

The grainy, blurry video of the police swarming the ditch wouldn't have told anyone anything. It was all reading between the lines at first—*second disappearance this month, possibly sex-related, victim young teenage girl last seen at a party in West Hills.* And then the details from one of the tabloid shows: throat cut, body unclothed. They do it every time there's a nice juicy murder. The St. Mary's angle was spread across the screen. *Schoolgirl Murder!*

The cops weren't even bent out of shape about the drugs and booze at the party. They didn't even ask. Just about Jack. Who was he? What exactly had he said? What had he been wearing? How tall was he? Did I know anything about him, anything at all?

Other kids had seen Chel leaving about midnight with a dark-haired guy, but nobody had talked to him. Only me, and I hadn't even said anything. All I'd done was listen to him and Chelsea flirt, and he hadn't said anything about himself at all.

Dad came into the kitchen and flicked the television off a little too hard, almost snapping the knob. I didn't realize I was hyperventilating until Consuela set flan in front of me, and clucked all over the kitchen, and made her special hot chocolate with cinnamon, too. She's been like that ever since she came to work for us, way before Mom left. I mean, who needs hot chocolate when it never gets cold down here? It's not called Sunny California for nothing.

It was almost like having Mom back.

Not really.

I finally went back up to my room and sat in the window seat with my knees pulled up. I was still kind of hungover. It was a bright sunny day. The wind had picked up, and the air was golden because of the dust and smoke wheezing through town. The Santa Anas had started.

My entire body was numb. I kept expecting my cell phone to ring Chel's song—"Just Say Yes," a forgettable number from a girl-band we'd both been gaga over in eighth grade even though we hadn't known each other. When we found out we both had loved the song it was like, whoa, Twilight Zone, and we were *meant* to be friends.

I kept wanting to pick it up and dial her and hear her voice. *Hey, bitch,* she'd say. *What the fuck you up to?*

The phone did ring. Bebe Marshall called. And Jenny Mailer. And JoJo Horschak—I didn't know she had my number. A couple other girls.

I turned the little crystal-dotted phone off. They weren't calling to wish me happy birthday or anything. It would be *ohmyGod* and *have you heard* and *did they tell you?*

Dad tapped at the door. "Honey?"

Uh-oh. I made a sound, staring out over the backyard. The pool glittered, hard blue. Tomorrow was Sunday. The landscapers would be out at some ungodly hour, clipping and mowing and pruning.

He opened the door halfway. He's so narrow and tall, that was all he needed. "I have a partner dinner at La Scala's, but I can cancel. Would you like—"

"Go ahead and go." I stared out the window. "It's Saturday. Consuela'll make tamales." Like always.

"I can cancel it. I can take you out instead."

Oh, Jesus, no. We would just sit and stare at each other, he would make awkward conversation, I would wish I was anywhere else. "It takes, like, months to get into La Scala's, Dad. Just go. I don't want to go out."

His thin, clean-shaven face flushed. He was trying to do the dad thing. Really, I got it. But Jesus. I hugged my knees even harder. My hair fell over my shoulders. I could still taste the beer from last night, even though I'd brushed my teeth.

"If you're sure." He waited a beat. His hair's cut a little longer than the usual attorney's buzz, because it's thick and wavy like mine. I think he counts the hairs in his brush every morning.

Chel'd thought so, too. A bubble of something hot and spiked burst right inside my chest.

"I'm sure. I really don't want to go anywhere."

He nodded. "I'll keep my cell phone on."

Oh, awkward. I hunched down even further. "Okay."

He left me alone after that, thank God. I waited and waited and finally took a shower, washing all the hangover and rancidness off me.

I didn't use the peach soap. It was on my windowsill, where I'd sat and stared at it. The lump of different soaps in my shower hurt when I scrubbed it over my skin, hard,

lather rising in fluffy streaks. Each week the cleaners wipe
under the multicolored lump, put together from pieces sto-
len from parties all over the county, and put it back.

I wonder what they think.

That night I dreamed.

*There were cliffs, and the sea. It crashed over and over again,
throwing up huge chunks of opalescent bubbles. I stood at the edge
looking down, and I was suddenly very sure Chelsea was down
there drowning. I couldn't hear her or see her, but I knew.*

*I stood looking down and the bubbles flushed pink. Then
they turned red, and a sickening smell belched up, blowing my
hair back. I tried to wake up but I couldn't. There was something
heavy on my chest, the breath all got squeezed out of me, and the
dream turned black until I . . .*

. . . opened my eyes to sunlight the next morning and
found out my period had started. I had a nasty sore throat,
too, and a hedge trimmer and lawnmower in the backyard
were drilling right through my head. I'd bled all through
my pajama bottoms and the whole thing made me so sick
I stumbled into my bathroom and threw up until I couldn't
retch anymore. Then I sat there on my knees on the cold tile
floor and cried.

By the next Friday I'd stopped bleeding. I had to go back to school, too. Dad got over the treating me like a delicate flower thing and told me so.

I had the same dream—ocean, drowning, bubbles—every night. I'd stopped bleeding but I was cramping, which wasn't normal. And I felt weird. Sore throat, a little tired, but nothing other than that.

I hadn't talked to anyone and it was like being a leper. Girls stared and whispered until blonde Bebe and redheaded Jenny showed up and stood on either side of me like body-guards. That reassured everyone that I was still part of the clique and there hadn't been any weird moving around in the pecking order. "Hey," Jen said. "How are you? Your phone's been off."

I wondered if she'd gotten *her* period yet. She looked perky. "My dad." I shrugged. "Lawyer stuff. He said not to talk to anyone until the cops . . ." I stopped there. You can only take a lie so far.

Bebe perked up. "You had to talk to the cops? How many times?"

Jenny elbowed her. "Jesus, Bebe. Try not to dance on the grave or anything."

That was something new. Usually Jenny and I watch while Bebe and Chelsea do the blonde follies.

But Chel was gone. And we were on the steps in front of St. Mary's pile of gray stone, the cross on top of the chapel's pointed roof glittering in the sun. There were ten minutes until first period, and everyone was looking at us.

"Sorry." Bebe dipped her head. Her long hair fell over one shoulder. She always looks like a shampoo commercial. She swung her bookbag. "We saw the guy, too. Chel looked drunk."

Christ. "She had a couple beers. Not enough to . . . you know."

"Maybe he slipped her something?" Jenny rolled her green eyes. The curls in her coppery hair aren't natural. I know because she smells like perm every once in a while. You just can't wash that smell out even if you get it done on a Friday afternoon and stay home all weekend. "Sorry. It's just, Jesus, you know?"

I did. "Let's go inside." Just then my cell phone started buzzing. I dug in my blazer pocket to fish it out, and cold fingers ran up my back. My stomach began to hurt.

The phone was tinkling "Just Say Yes." I flipped it open and stared in disbelief.

Chel. Four little letters on the LCD display.

"Who's calling?" Bebe craned her neck to see, but I hit the power button and held it down. The song died, strangled, and her name winked out.

"I don't know," I said. It was the truth. My fingers felt cold, even though the sun was blazing down on us. Getting from air-conditioned car to air-conditioned school is sometimes the worst part of the day, and everything was full of dust. The wind was up, teasing at everyone's hair. I'd zapped myself twice on the fridge this morning trying to find something I felt like eating. "Let's go in."

Bebe took the hint, and we all started up the steps. "There's a party at Kell's tonight."

"Tragic," I mumbled. People were staring. I fought the urge to hunch my shoulders. You can't ever look weak while walking in to school. It's blood in the water.

Friday night another blonde girl disappeared. Amy Macanzito. They found her Sunday morning. Throat cut. Body naked. *Schoolgirl Murders*, the paper and the TV blared. It was official.

The next Thursday, Dad was working late and Consuela had retreated to her room with Mexican wrestling on her television. It was a warm fall night, the wind full of dust and smoke but falling off a little around dusk. I plunged into the pool, stroked out to the middle, turned over on my back, and just floated. The stars came out in ones and twos.

If Chel was here we'd be sitting on the concrete edge, dangling our legs and talking desultorily. The winds made everyone nervous. Sometimes during them you heard sirens all night, all over town. People go crazy listening to that low moan day and night. Chel said it was bad electricity that drove them nuts.

My stomach trembled. I'd pushed my dinner around my plate, but Consuela hadn't said anything beyond offering me a double helping of dessert. She was awful quiet lately. I knew she was worried by the way she kept making my favorites.

High scudding clouds hung like veils. Light drained away from the sky while I lay floating. My cheeks were wet, but it didn't matter in the pool. Hot tears beaded up and vanished in the chlorinated water. My hair was going to frizz big-time.

After a while I moved. Water lapped. The pool was lit, a jewel of blue, its reflections starring the back of the house in a wide slice. It looked like the house had jazzed up for a party. I thought of bringing the dish soap out and dumping it in here.

She's just tragic, I heard Chelsea say. I swam slowly for the side of the pool. I could haul myself out and sit there, let the warm wind dry me.

It took a while to reach the side. I put my hands up, got ready to pull myself out of the water, and the just-trimmed bushes moved. There was a flash of white.

I froze. Water ran in warm trickles down my neck, my ears clearing out. I blinked, but it was dark and the shadow-dazzle of the pool made everything shift weird. I was still there, hanging onto the side of the pool, when he *appeared.*

I floundered over backward. Water gushed. My feet found the pool wall and I *pushed*, hard, and made it away. I got to the middle of the pool and stopped, staring goggle-eyed while trying to stay above the water.

He hadn't moved, crouching easily on the concrete lip. Same sneakers, same worn designer jeans, same white shirt. Same olive skin, same curly hair, same dark eyes fixed on me. Only now a spark of crimson showed in each eye. When he blinked, the red—it was like a little LED light right in his pupil—winked cheerfully at me.

"Jesus Christ," I whispered. The water splashed. Goose-bumps marched up my skin.

"Nope." He grinned. The necklace was a gold chain and a tooth, startlingly white against his throat. "Jack. Remember?"

I treaded water. If he jumped in, maybe I could make it to the steps in the shallow end. My heart pounded so hard even my fingers felt it. "What are you doing here?"

"Visiting you." He cocked his head a little. His hands dangled as he crouched, and those red spots in his eyes were so unfunny. "I've been thinking about you."

"Are you going to kill me?" It was out before I could stop myself.

He stopped, staring at me. Those red dots blinked, dimmed. "Of course not," he said finally. "Don't be stupid."

I didn't bother to point out that it wasn't a stupid question, everything considered. "What did you do to Chelsea?"

His head-tilt got more pronounced. He looked just like a cat staring at something confusing. "Chelsea?" He said the word like it was foreign.

"My friend." My arms and legs were heavy, treading water that suddenly felt far too cold. The wind picked up, making a dry whooshing sound. "At the party."

"Ah." He grinned, white teeth flashing, and I began to feel like my head was too heavy. "Did she not enjoy herself?"

My heart pounded in my chest. My arms and legs stopped working and my vision squeezed down to a pinhole.

Because his teeth weren't just so pearly white they glowed. The overlarge canines curved sharply down, just like in a bad horror movie, and those red dots in his eyes dilated. My body stiffened, jolted back, and the pounding filled my skull. The dry Santa Ana wind rushed in, and I sank under the water with a grateful exhalation. I'd never fainted in my life before. That was the first time.

I heard a splash like a body hitting water, and then the sound of the wind filled everything with funny brown darkness.

I came to lying on concrete. My eyes opened and I saw the stars. The lights were still on. My throat hurt, and I was out of the pool. My skin was drying and my hair was, too, wet curls raveling up into dry frizz. I pushed myself up on my elbows and found out I was alone. And still alive. My heart still beat.

There were drops of dried blood on my chest, where the swimsuit didn't cover.

The next week, my phone rang again, the tinkling little notes of "Just Say Yes" filling my room as I sat on my bed with my trig book open. I was ignoring my homework and trying to do it at the same time. I snatched it up and hit the "dismiss" button, then thought maybe I should tell someone.

Right after that Bebe called. "We're going to the Rose. Come with."

I looked at the window. It was dark and the winds were still blowing. The stars burned dryly wherever you could see them. "Got homework."

"You've been, like, a hermit for a week. We're kidnapping you. Get dressed."

Yeah, no shit I'd been a hermit. I was inside before dark every day, and I stayed there. It was like being a prisoner in my own house. "We?"

"Me and Jen and JoJo. Come on." Someone giggled in the background, and the doorbell rang. I heard Consuela yell *Uno momento!* as she headed for the door. "We're at your house, bitch. Get dressed." She probably meant to sound cheerful, but there was a warning in her tone.

Translation: I was falling down on my social bargains, and I wasn't going to be part of their crowd much longer if I didn't snap out of it.

So what could I do? I threw on a pair of jeans and a cami, brushed my hair, stuffed my ID and some cash into my bra, and headed downstairs.

"*There* she is!" Jenny sang. Her pupils were dilated—she was high as fuck. Bebe giggled, and JoJo flashed me a half-ass gang sign. "I'm on the rag! Hey, your hair looks great. What have you done with it?"

"Congrats." I whipped her the finger and all three of them broke up. JoJo was high, too. I could smell the weed on both of them. "Hey, Consuela, I'm going out. I'll be back."

She held her pink print robe closed with one hand. "Should I tell your father?" Her tone hovered between worried and unable-to-push-it-because-I'm-an-employee.

"He's working late, he won't care." Actually, I thought he was probably with his secretary, but it didn't matter. He wasn't home. That was the main thing.

"Be careful, *mija*." The cross at her throat glittered golden.

"Wow. Tragic." JoJo rolled her eyes.

"Let's go." I skipped down off the stairs and headed for them, and they scattered out the front door like birds. Jen put her arm over my shoulder. She smelled like Chanel and powder deodorant, and the heavy musk of weed.

"Dude, you've got a hickey." She blinked at my neck. I almost shoved her off the front step, the dust-laden wind pulled at my hair, and we all piled into Bebe's Mini Cooper. As soon as we did, JoJo handed me a joint and we lit up, Bebe started the car, and I began smoking like there was no tomorrow.

I couldn't wait to be buzzed.

Dancing is tragic, but on nights when there's no parties it's what we've got. So we toked up good and hard before we went in, but not hard enough to make us just want to sit in the car. It's a fine art.

So we were trance-dancing, all in a circle, and Jenny was looking pretty happy for a girl who was on the rag. I didn't blame her. Giving birth to another Marty would be *truly* tragic.

The Rose was a loud throbbing womb of lights flashing, fake smoke, kids crowding. We spent about an hour in there before getting the munchies and swarming the bathroom so

Jen could replace her plug. We spilled out onto the street and JoJo lit a cigarette, despite the fat-assed bouncer glowering at her. "Move *along!*" he yelled, and Jenny whipped him the finger. She even kissed the tip of it before she blew it at him. We all laughed and moved down the street.

It wasn't a long way to Druby's Diner, where all the kids went for noshing after the Rose. I had my arm over Jen's shoulders and we were both singing, just what I didn't know. Bebe was boogeying, and JoJo flicked her cigarette out into the street. "Fire hazard!" she crowed, and that broke us all up pretty good. I let go of Jen and she hooked up with Bebe instead, both of them doing some sort of dance step. There were trembling coronas of light around every streetlight, dust spilling through them. I stopped to take a look and they all went be-bopping on. I figured I'd catch up with them at Druby's. They were my ride home, after all.

And as if I knew he was somehow going to be there, Jack stepped out of the shadows on the other side of the street. Golden lamplight ran along his curls. He stood there, hands in his pockets, staring at me.

Same white shirt. Same jeans. Same hair, same nose, same eyes. Only they didn't have red LEDs in them now.

He stepped down off the curb like he had all the time in the world and ambled across the street. I half expected a car to come along and mash him, but nothing did. Of course it wouldn't. He was too sure.

He was too real. Everything else was paper and plastic, and he was something else. It was like a hole in the world where something behind it was peeking through.

I stood there. Waves of hot and cold went down me. JoJo yelled, and it sounded very far away.

He reached the sidewalk. Three steps and he was next to me. His hand closed around my arm, and he pushed me around on one heel and we were walking right into an alley opening up off Elm Street.

Why they call it Elm I don't know. There's not an elm tree for miles.

He kept walking. It got darker. All the breath whooshed out of me. I sucked it back in. "What are you?" I sounded high, and squeaky, and scared out of my mind.

Jack gave me a sideways glance. "You know what I am."

"What are you going to do?" My legs weren't quite working right. He didn't seem to mind.

"I'm going to give you a present." He stopped. As if it was the most natural thing in the world, he turned and put his arms around me. I was rigid. He sighed into my hair. "I've been watching you."

"What did you do to Chelsea?" It took all the air I had to get the sentence out.

"I tried her out. But I don't like blondes." A small laugh into my hair. His breath was warm. "They told me I'd get lonely after a while. They said to be careful. You're perfect."

Nobody had ever said anything remotely like that to me before. My heart was pounding. The waves of hot and cold intensified, each one shaking me a little. I made some sort of tiny sound.

"You, I can change." His lips brushed mine. His breath smelled like peppermints and smoky desire. He rested his forehead against mine, like he could read my mind by pressing our skulls together. "But you have to do something, sweetheart."

"What?" I was drowning.

"You have to say yes." He leaned against me, his arms over my shoulders, our foreheads touching, and everything else was so far away. Our bodies fit together. The only other real person in a cardboard world, and he was standing right in front of me.

Had he held Chelsea this way? Did he do it before he . . .

My brain stopped working. His head dipped. He kissed my cheek. Nuzzled at my jaw. "Say yes," he whispered. "Say it."

What else did I have to say? There was nothing I could do. I was still following Chelsea.

It was too late to back out now.

"Yes," I whispered, and the teeth, long and sharp, drove into my throat. I jerked, my body finally realizing that I was driving it right off the edge of the cliff, but his arms were like steel bands and he still smelled of peppermint and sweetness. I understood why she'd gone with him.

Anyone would.

C⁓

Sunlight. Hurt. Stinging my eyes. I blinked. My alarm clock was making a horrible noise and my throat hurt. I managed to hit the snooze button and lay there, stunned.

What the hell?

I blinked again. The ceiling blurred. My cell phone rang again, vibrating on my nightstand. I fumbled for it.

It was Jenny. She didn't waste any time. "Jesus! Where the *hell* did you go last night? We freaked the *fuck* out! What *happened?*"

Oh, shit. I wasn't dead. My head hurt like a steel spike was driving right through it. I fumbled around some more until I came up with sunglasses and slid them on. "My dad called." The lie came out hoarse and natural. "He was insane. I had to ditch and go home."

"And you couldn't call? Or, like, walk five steps to tell us?" She was really worked up.

"Jesus, Jen, you know my dad." She didn't, but it was a good line. "He said to come home right-fucking-now. I jumped in a cab. My phone was dying anyway. What's your damage?"

It was the wrong thing to say. But Christ I was tired of putting up with the shit. And didn't she have any fucking clue that last night . . .

Jack.

My brain froze up briefly. I smelled peppermints, copper, hot desire, and felt his arms around me again. A bolt of heat went through me. Consuela was stirring downstairs. I smelled the bacon before it hit the pan and began to sizzle. I heard her humming to herself.

"Well, excuse the fuck out of me." But Jen sounded oddly unrighteous. Kind of deflated. "Are you coming to school today? Did you just wake up?"

"Just." I checked the time. My throat hurt like hell. I sounded like I had a cold. "I'll be there. See you in class." And then I hung up and tossed the phone back on the nightstand, flung my arm over my eyes.

Oh Jesus. I wasn't dead.

What was going to happen now?

When you've got a big heaping helping of who-gives-a-fuck, school loses a lot of its importance. And worrying about your friends tossing you off the top of the food chain loses a lot of its snap, too.

But a funny thing happens when you don't care anymore. Suddenly they can't get enough of you.

Was this how Chelsea always felt? Take it or leave it, who the hell cares, fuck off? JoJo and Bebe both fell over themselves trying to make me talk. They gossiped and Jenny fell back into watching. It was exhausting to be the one they were trying to impress. JoJo in particular would *not shut up*, and during class time the teachers were talking on and on about shit that didn't matter. None of it mattered.

Because he'd bitten me. The two scab-marks on my throat, small rough spots under my fingertips when I realized I was touching them, felt hot. Infected.

And I wasn't dead. I wasn't in a ditch with my legs spread and my throat cut.

Trig class gave me some time to think. I doodled aimlessly on my paper, sometimes glancing up at the crucifix over the door as Sister Lucia droned on about the wonders of mathematics. I took notes, too, whenever I could focus enough to hear what she was saying.

I wasn't dead. My throat hurt, a dry sandy pain.

It was near the end of trig when the idea took shape, slowly, under the surface of utter panic. I guess from the outside I looked calm, but everything was whirling inside me. Like the winds, whistling sharply around the corners of the building. The low moan ran under my thoughts, scattering them like the dust particles that had spun through the circles of lamplight last night.

But the thought wouldn't go away, and it finally shouted itself loud enough to be heard over the wind, just as Sister Lucia said my name.

"Are you ill?" Her eyebrows were up, her wrinkled mouth set in a thin line.

"I don't feel good," I croaked. Convincingly, even.

She wrote me out a pass to go visit the nurse. "Lucky," JoJo said softly as I picked up my bag and scooped my book and notepaper together.

I almost replied *Bite me*, but the words died in my burning throat.

I didn't visit the nurse, either. I got off school grounds the way Chel and I always had when we skipped, flagged down a cab on Charter Street, and went home. Consuela was out shopping, so nobody saw me when I drank two bottles of Evian and went out to the gardening shed. The water sloshed uneasily in my protesting stomach.

I found what I was looking for, and stood staring at it for a long time before getting down to work. I almost ripped one of my fingernails off and a splinter the size of Texas rammed into the meat of my left hand. When I pulled it out, a trickle of blood followed, and I clamped my mouth over it before I could think twice.

I came back to myself on my knees, sucking at my hand, my hips tilting back and forth as I rocked and moaned a little. The metallic tang of blood slid across the dry sand filling my throat, sharpening the thirst. And I surprised myself by bursting into tears. I sniveled until the snot ran down my face while I finished working, then I got back in the house and cleaned up before Consuela got home. I scrubbed at my hands for a long time, the lather building up, and the bubbles went down the drain with a wet chuckling sound.

"You look sick, *mija*." Consuela put her wrist against my forehead. "You go to bed early, *ay*?" She set the plate down in front of me, and the sight of food made me feel like horking like that bulimic bitch JoJo.

Dad stuck a forkful of steak in his mouth, chewed. His eyes were on me. When he finally swallowed, he set his fork down and took a sip of wine. "You do look pale. Maybe you should go to bed early instead of running around with your friends."

I hung my head and tried to look repentant. "Yeah, I think so. My stomach's messed up."

He stared at me like he knew what I was up to. Consuela shuffled out of the dining room.

The sun was going down. I tried not to stare at the window.

"Eat," Dad said, finally. "You're coming up on your seventeenth birthday, aren't you?"

I nodded. My hair fell forward. I swiped it back, took a drink of milk, and immediately wished I hadn't.

"You've got your permit, and you'll have your license soon. Have you thought about the kind of car you want?" He smiled like it was Christmas, pleased with himself.

I made all the appropriate noises. I told him a Volvo like Mom used to have would be nice, and watched him flinch. I ate as much as I could, and when he was finished I fled upstairs, turned up the music in my room, and threw up everything in a curdled rush as the sun slid toward the horizon and the wind rasped, moaned, and whistled.

When it was done I rested my feverish forehead against the cool porcelain of the toilet. It felt good. I cleaned myself up and felt a little better now that I didn't have the food weighing me down, and it was getting to be dusk. So I brushed my teeth, gagging at the mint in the toothpaste, and put on a pair of jeans and a cami, and went out in the backyard. Consuela was washing dishes and my dad was in his home office on the phone.

Nobody saw me leave.

The gardening shed was full of cobwebs, the smell of oil and grass clippings, and weird shadows. The riding mower hunched under a tarp, for those times when Dad got a bug up his ass about the lawn. I sat on an old concrete bench that had been hauled in here probably before I was born, and waited.

Night filled the one little window. It was hot and the wind moaned, flinging dust everywhere. My hair filled with electricity, but the waves were springy. Go figure, the day I feel like shit warmed over is the day I have good hair.

I waited, chewing on my fingernail. The scab on my left palm throbbed, and the two little puncture scabs on my throat sent a zing through me every time I moved.

The door quivered. I swallowed hard and sat up straight. *Lift your chin, sweetheart, it takes years off.*

Goddamn.

"And what are you doing in here?" The red dots were back in his eyes. He shut the door casually. "You've said your good-byes, I guess. Right?"

He sounded so *sure*. I curled my left hand around the wood. "Yeah."

"You certainly don't disappoint. Are you thirsty, darling? Say yes."

Just say yes. Sourness filled my mouth. "Yes."

"Well, come on. There's a whole world out there." His eyes glittered and his teeth gleamed. The fangs all but glowed.

I held up my right hand and smiled. It felt like wood on my frozen face. "Okay."

He stepped closer. His fingers closed around mine. "You know, as a rendezvous, this isn't—"

I jerked at him *hard* with my right hand, brought the stake up in my left. It was braced against the wall, a long round piece of wood left over from the bonsai experiments that had been here when we moved in. It had taken a little bit of hacking with a rusted machete before the end was sharpened enough. It went in with a meaty sound that would have made me throw up again if I wasn't already so sick.

Jack's face went slack. The red lights in his eyes dimmed, but his teeth champed together twice. His head dropped like he'd just fallen asleep, and he almost fell on me. The end of the long-ass stake skritched against the wall of the shed, and I landed on my knees. He folded to the side, landed slumped against the bulk of the riding mower, and a long rattling hiss like an angry snake filled the shed, overpowering the sound of the wind.

I let out a coughing sob. Stumbled for the door. The stake whapped against things as his body convulsed. I don't know what I was expecting. I thought maybe he'd turn to dust, or explode, or something. But he just kept making that hissing sound, and the end of the stake kept hitting things. It seemed to last forever before he fell down between the riding mower and the shed wall, the stake pointing up before cocking over to the side. His legs made one final little dancing movement and then were still.

Deathly still.

It was like a nightmare where you can't run fast enough. My dumb fingers closed around the doorknob. I ran, the door slamming shut behind me, lungs bursting and heart pounding, and made it into the house. I shut the pool door, locked it, and stepped quick and soft up the stairs until I reached my room.

As a plan, it kind of sucked. But it was all I had. And here in the house the lights were bright and they were all on. I slumped against my bedroom door, hyperventilating. My throat throbbed. When I put my hand up to touch the little puncture wounds, my fingers came away wet and red. I sucked on them while I stumbled to the bathroom. I had to pee like damn.

"Tragic," I whispered around my fingers, and giggled. "I'm so tragic."

It took a long time before I could stop crying. The divots in my neck stopped bleeding after a little bit, re-scabbed, and I stood in the shower for a long time, shaking and shuddering.

I tossed the mashed-together chunks of soap in the garbage. Faint bubbles on its wet surface gleamed before they popped.

Then I went to bed and I dreamed of Chel. Only she was on the riding mower, and she was cutting down banks of bubbles and leaving a river of blood behind her. And when I woke up the next morning, I was still thirsty.

Consuela flipped the television on. "You eat," she told me, sternly, her eyebrows coming together. "Don't starve yourself, *mija*."

I eyed the eggs and potatoes, the bacon, the toast. My stomach turned into a knot and the news came on. I picked up the glass of orange juice. Dad was already at work.

"—the so-called Schoolgirl Murders," the television said. Consuela reached for the knob.

"Don't!" The orange juice slid from my hand. The glass didn't break, but half of it slopped into my plate and she gave me a reproachful look. "Sorry. I'm sorry."

She whisked the plate away and the television kept yapping.

"Again, the chief of police has just issued a statement. Theodore Michael Briggs, a twenty-four-year old handyman in the Valley, has just been charged with the Schoolgirl Murders." The screen filled with a mug shot of a dark-haired man with a narrow face. He didn't look anything like Jack, really, but his hair was dark and curly and he was skinny.

Consuela started mopping up the orange juice. I stared at the television screen.

"The murders have held the entire city in a grip of fear," the blonde anchorwoman intoned as the picture shrank and retreated to the upper right-hand corner of the screen. "Police arrested Briggs in the company of a young girl from St. Mary's Academy, where two of the victims attended school. The girl's parents are calling it a narrow escape—"

"*Mija?*" Consuela said softly.

"A source close to the investigation says Briggs was found with several items belonging to the victims, including four cell phones—"

"Holy *fuck*," I whispered, and slid off my stool. Consuela called my name, sharply, but I was already at the back door and running for the shed.

When I got there the door was open, and there was a dark stain on the cement floor. But no stake.

And no body. The shed was hot, airless—and empty.

The wind is up. It mouths at the edges of the house and the air-conditioning is working overtime. It's a fall heat wave, ninety degrees in the shade and no hope of a break for a while. And with the wind, well, everyone's crazy. The news was full of rapes, fires, other stuff.

"At least they caught that bastard," Dad said before he kissed my cheek and went out for another partner dinner. Consuela fussed at me. I tried eating, ran upstairs and threw it all up afterward. I didn't even fucking care.

I'm sitting on my bed, staring at the window. Sunlight is draining out of the sky. The wind moans, and moans. The two little wounds on my throat are pulsing-hot. The inside of my throat is on fire, and part of why I ran upstairs after dinner is because I could hear Consuela's heart working, each chamber throbbing open and clapping shut.

I could smell the blood in her veins.

It smells good. Even now, upstairs, with my door closed and the lights on, it smells so *good*.

It's almost night. They expect the Santa Anas to blow themselves out soon. I have my hands knotted together into fists. I'm waiting. My entire body aches.

I should have said no. Jesus Christ, I should have said no.

I'm thirsty.

And I'm waiting. God only knows what he'll do when he comes back.

But the thing that really scares me?

Is the idea that he might not.

Letters to Romeo

NANCY HOLDER

In fair Verona, where we lay our scene:

Romeo attacked the old man in the foyer of the villa's home movie theater while busy servants decorated the room with festoons of orange-tree flowers, dried pomegranates, and silver leaves. He bent the drugged-out, half-dead bag of bones backward beneath the hanging pots of deadly nightshade and sunk in his fangs. Immediately he spit out the blood. It was contaminated with tetrodox—rank, disgusting. It rendered its victims paralytic. Sometimes it stopped hearts. It was a chemical sister of the poison Friar Lawrence had given to Juliet, to fake her own death.

"Who did this?" Romeo shouted. "Who dared?"

The servants kept to the shadows, rats fearing the king of the beasts—Romeo Montague, seven hundred years a nobleman of Verona, seven centuries the lover of Juliet Capulet, and a vampire.

The stone coat of arms of the House of Montague, which had adorned his family's crypt until the nineteenth century, hung over his head like a crown. Fashionable apartments now stood where the palazzo had sprawled lavishly down the hillside. In fact, that was where he had found the old man, swaying in a doorway, drunk, starving, and crying for his cat—which, it turned out, had died five years before.

Romeo had invited the miserable old man home to have dinner, and he had fed him well, too—better than he himself had eaten, when he had still eaten, though he was the only son of a noble family and therefore accustomed to the best. Romeo wasn't being kind; he did it to fatten up the old man's blood, so to speak, so that his own blood when he shared it would be full and rich. He wanted his love to have the best—or at the least, the best that he could give her under the circumstances.

The old man would be Romeo's antipasto; it was Romeo's intention that a slew of better dishes—healthier veins— would follow. Until Juliet was changed, he had to lay low. It was difficult to hunt in these days of cell phones, Google Earth, and security surveillance cameras—especially since he didn't show up on any of them—and Romeo had been very distracted of late. Distracted meant careless, and vampires could not afford to be careless.

But he wasn't so much careless as lovesick. The people of the 1300s had believed that love at first sight was a kind of lunacy, and Romeo now believed that they had been entirely correct. His love for Juliet Capulet had driven him mad. Imagine loving, wanting, for seven hundred years. Living the life of a fiend to pursue the sweetest of angels. Believing in God and in magic and then in nothing and then believing again, and then losing faith in everything. The unrelenting loneliness. How did one still hope, after the first century, the second?

That was the nature of love. Utter madness.

Romeo wore a black silk shirt, black jeans, and black boots. His black hair was cut close to his head, and his cheeks were scruffy with five-o'clock shadow. He had dark eyebrows, dark eyes, and darker lashes. Women swooned over him. But he didn't take advantage—didn't kiss them, didn't kill them. He was married.

He was married!

Juliet. Her name was the answer to centuries of prayer, and bargaining. During bad times—wars, famines, and the continued, utter absence of any sign of her—Romeo assumed that if there was a God, He despised him. Why else deny him his wife, when he had suffered so much for love of her?

But he was alone no longer. Claire Johnson, the reincarnation of Juliet, had been living in his house for six months, and tomorrow night, she would be fifteen years old. Back in the day, Lord Capulet had betrothed her to Count Paris, insisting that he wait until she turned fifteen to marry her. So this time, he would wait for the magic number, fifteen, in hopes that things would fare better.

Drumming his fingers on the table while the old man devoured a steak and a plate of pasta, Romeo had asked him questions. His staff bustled everywhere, putting up canopies of white silk and lilies, dusting, sweeping. Polishing the silverware and the crystal. Preparing a sumptuous feast for her last meal as a human.

When he was certain that no one would miss the toothless old *signor*, he had attacked.

And now this . . . outrage.

"Who poisoned his blood?" he thundered.

Snarling, he let the body fall to the floor. Night's candles had all burned out; the oldster's face was as gray and pale as a dead rat, and his bones cracked as he hit the hard marble.

Tomorrow night, he thought, staring at the drugged man's blank eyes, *she'll feed for the first time. And I was about to suck down poison. If from my unholy blood, she takes offense . . .*

He rammed his fist into the wall as his fangs retracted. He was hungry and angry; was he, the lord of this place, to be denied a simple meal?

"Romeo," Lucenzo said, bowing low as he approached. He was Romeo's lieutenant, and he had hopes of becoming a vampire himself. "What's the matter?"

"Someone gave this man tetrodox," Romeo said.

Lucenzo's dark Italian eyes widened. "Surely not," he countered. "Who would dare to do such a thing in your house?"

"Who, indeed? Someone who has more will to be kind than to live?"

"He must have had it before he came here."

"Impossible. Where would he have gotten it?" He glared at Lucenzo. "Find out. And when you do, bring him, or her, to me."

Lucenzo grimaced. "Romeo, it's one night before the *Signora's* birthday. She's not used to . . . there's so much she's had to adjust to. A death like that would shock her."

"She knows what I am. What I do. What I'm like."

But did she? He had explained. He had even fed in front of her. But he had softened all of it—using Lucenzo as a willing donor, whom he left very much alive. Swearing a silent vow that, with her at his side, he would return to the gentle hunt he had employed when he'd first been turned. Once more, he would become the soft youth he had been before her death—and not the angry, tormented—

—*Monster*—

"I won't kill whoever did it," he informed Lucenzo. "But there *will* be consequences."

"*Sì*," Lucenzo said.

"And clean it up." Romeo gestured to the old man. "He's still alive. Take him back to his doorway. He'll think it was all a dream, with all that tetrodox in his bloodstream."

"Of course," Lucenzo said.

Romeo turned his back on the mess and slammed down the hall. Livid, he pulled out his cell phone. And there he saw his wallpaper picture of Claire, grinning at him between glasses of Chianti. Her hair was wound into two little top-knots, and she was wearing the Italian *Twilight* T-shirt she had bought as a joke.

His anger softened. In the past, he had used a poison very like tetrodox to paralyze his victims and numb them from pain. Friar Lawrence had taught him to distill it. But it had been a pain to make. He'd had to buy hundreds of gallons of the puffer fish derivative and store it in his crypt. And it fouled the blood and made him sick. Sometimes he hallucinated. So ultimately he had banned it, although he hadn't disposed of it. What if someone beyond the world of his villa discovered it, and traced it back to him?

When he'd awakened that evening, he'd impulsively carried one gallon of the stuff from the crypt up to the kitchen. He'd thought to show it to Claire, as she seemed quite intrigued by the idea that seven hundred years ago, "she" had drunk poison to feign her own death. There were servants everywhere, preparing for Juliet's big night, and he had discussed using a sedative and painkillers for her transformation with Lucenzo. They'd chatted about the tetrodox in the kitchen within earshot of the cook and a dozen other of Romeo's staff. Maybe someone had gotten confused and thought he meant to use it on the old man. Still, one did not make such assumptions in the home of a vampire.

He looked down at Claire's picture again. Was she counting down the hours, the way he was? Seven hundred years of waiting. *Seven hundred.*

ILY. R, he texted. He smirked. Look at the son of the House of Montague, texting. He wasn't big on it. There was no grace in it.

The era Romeo and Juliet had been born in had been violent, yes, yet graceful in its way. Duty and honor were as real as love at first sight. The twenty-first century was more complicated, with murky rules, coarse language, and coarser behavior. There was sex everywhere. If their story had begun now, instead of back then, they would never have had to kill themselves for the sake of their innocent passion. Very few people these days believed in the kind of love they had—a love that conquered the grave.

He waited. She didn't text back.

J? he added, with a flash of irritation. Or was it fear?

There's nothing to fear, he reminded himself. *She is Juliet. My search is over.* But the fear wouldn't go away. It washed over him like the horror of finding himself buried in unhallowed ground, behind the sanctuary of his family's vault. He was a suicide, after all, destined for hell, and a suicide did not deserve to lie with the faithful sons and daughters of the church.

He balled his fists. Sometimes he wanted to lock Juliet in her room, as men had done back in his time to protect their women. The world outside was dangerous. Look what had happened to Juliet herself, sneaking out to meet him. Her father had been too permissive. And his daughter had come to grief.

Nothing could have stopped us, he thought. *Not locks, nor fathers. We were fortune's fools.*

He'd thought long and hard about recapturing those days for her. About making sure nothing happened to her. He could move them to a more old-fashioned, isolated villa—a place in the Italian countryside, where people lived slower, simpler lives. Maybe in Mantua; he hadn't minded his brief exile there. The sunsets there had brought tears to his eyes.

Mantua was where things had gone wrong. Where he had not received the letter informing him that she was lying in a stupor in the Capulet tomb, waiting for him to wake her with a kiss. The architect of that fiasco, Friar Lawrence, had promised she would one day return to her beloved. Insisted that he'd arranged for it to happen. But the old magician had died a failure in that as well, refusing at the end to be saved from death in the way he had saved Romeo.

"Better to die," the old man had said, gasping, "than to become like you."

"Tormented," Romeo had whispered through his fangs. "As you made me."

For centuries Romeo had roamed the world, seeking her. *Juliet, Juliet, where art thou, Juliet?* Paying magicians, then torturing them, to force them to do what Friar Lawrence had promised. Studying in monasteries, fasting, scourging himself. Praying, threatening. Friar Lawrence had sworn that she'd return. But she had not.

His despair was the cause of his temper. Take love from him, and light was absent. He was a vampire, a creature of darkness, whose black deeds were born in a heart that was dying of loneliness, and regret.

Then, by love's light wings, he'd found her—on Facebook. His search engine had pointed to her after she had quoted the Shakespeare play about them. Then he had seen the confirming crescent moon on her shoulder. Not a tattoo, but a real birthmark, like Juliet's. The chances of finding her in such a seemingly random manner made him wonder if there was a God after all, one that could perform miracles.

He had long ago ceased to believe in magic, though Friar Lawrence had sworn on his immortal soul that magic would bring her back. After the first fifty years of waiting, and then the first century, Romeo probably would have killed the old monk-cum-sorcerer for the sin of false hope, if Lawrence hadn't died first.

Juliet. Giulietta. Her contemporary name was Claire Johnson, and she lived in Tampa. He sent her email messages and chatted with her online, making up reasons for why he wouldn't use a webcam. The truth was, he wouldn't be visible on it. It took him several months to reveal the truth.

She had been convinced much more quickly than he would ever have imagined. Convinced, and accepting.

"I haven't had a great life," she wrote. *"My parents were horrible to me. I ran away when I was fourteen. I've been on the streets so long, seen so many things. . . Sounds like you have, too."*

Then Lucenzo had flown to Florida in a private jet to collect her. Romeo had paced, slept, fed, and paced some more. He knew he shouldn't expect his lady to wear velvets and silks, but it was still a bit of a shock when she arrived in Italy tanned, wearing capris and an empire-waisted paisley blouse, earbuds in, and chewing gum. Shaking, he held himself back as she walked into the villa, gazing around, saying, "Wow." And then when she saw him, raising her eyebrows.

Lucenzo had said the only difference was his paleness. And when the bloodlust was on him, the red eyes and fangs. But she looked a little shocked.

"Hey," she said. She smiled. It was a weak smile, but it was there. "Romeo."

No curtsy, no courtly language. Just "Hey, Romeo." But it was enough. He trembled, so badly; tears spilled down his cheeks, and she came to him then, saying, "Oh, wow, shit," and she put her arms around him.

"Juliet," he whispered brokenly. "My life, my wife."

She put her head on his chest. They communed in silence; he felt her soul pouring into him.

"You don't have a heartbeat," she said.

"Yes, I do. It beats outside my chest," he replied, daring to put his hand on her hair. He breathed in her scent—gum, coconut oil, Juicy Couture perfume—and shut his eyes tightly.

"That's so sweet," she told him. "*You're* sweet."

"I'm not," he replied. And he felt despicable, horrible. But he'd had to do all the evil things that he'd done, to live for her. What if he hadn't grabbed onto life and wrestled it from the catacombs? What if she had come back, and not found him waiting? What would have happened to her own sweet soul?

He stirred, feeling panicky at the mere thought of failing her. But he had done it, he reminded himself. She was here.

Still . . . maybe not Mantua. He was the one longing for the old days, while she didn't even remember them. He'd put himself on hold for centuries, not living in the world but lingering in the shadows, as he waited for her, searched for her, performed unspeakable rites to obtain her.

Unspeakable. He spared half a glance in the direction of the old man as two lackeys laid him on a blanket and the others resumed cleaning the room.

Romeo walked into his study. He leaned against the black glass brick surrounding the enormous tank of tropical fish. Then he opened the drawer in his ebony desk and took out a small octagonal box covered with Italian mosaics. He lifted the lid and studied the dust inside.

One letter, sent to him via her nurse. No one hand wrote anything now. It was all electronic, immediate and fleeting. But she had sent him reassurance of her love, after he had wooed her on her balcony, after her family's party.

> *Romeo, oh, Romeo,*
> *My bounty is as boundless as the sea,*
> *My love as deep.*
> *The more I give to thee, the more I have,*
> *For both are infinite.*
>
> *Juliet*

He dipped his forefinger in the dust. He hadn't known how to preserve the note, and it had disintegrated. But he had kept it with him always, and the words were engraved on his heart. He had spoken the words aloud to Juliet in her new incarnation as Claire. She had giggled, then smiled and put in her earbuds.

Wooing women was different then.

Death had been even more different.

Verona, 1336

Blackness. Romeo floated in it, as if he had no body. It was cold, and his face was wet. Was he crying?

The last thing he remembered was the sight of his dead love, his new wife, Juliet. After Romeo had been banished for killing her cousin, she had died of grief. For him: the poison had been very painful, but the agony had been short.

Why, then, was he floating in darkness? He was a suicide. Was this hell?

Then Romeo realized he was lying on his back in a ditch in the cold, soggy ground, and mud coated his face, his chest, and his arms. He'd been buried in the earth, not in his family's crypt. Buried alive? Stars, what punishment was this for the sin of suicide?

Attempted suicide, as evidently he had failed. He wanted to rage against his fate. Then something was thrown over his face—rough cloth; someone lifted him up in strong arms. He tried to speak, but he could only groan softly.

I'm alive, he thought. Then, *Let me die.*

Then he sank into blackness.

After a time, there was more movement, something pressing down on him. Someone covering him. As he gathered his thoughts, a hot poker burned his neck; fire shot through his veins and coursed through his body. The pain was unimaginable, like being plunged into eternal flames, the hellfires of damnation.

He screamed. Then a hand covered his mouth. In the blurred glare of a torch, Friar Lawrence's moon-shaped face came into view. The friar's heavy brows met over the bridge of his large nose as he stared down at Romeo. Someone was standing behind the friar, but Romeo couldn't tell who.

He was no longer cold. But his heart . . . what was wrong with his heart? It ached. And he was so thirsty.

"Hssst," Friar Lawrence said. "You must be silent."

The friar glanced backward, over his own shoulder. "Do you have the . . . blood?" he asked.

"Sì," said a voice, low and deep.

Romeo fought against the friar's hand again, and the friar bent down and grabbed Romeo's head with his other hand. The other figure remained in darkness.

"You must make no sound, for we have very little time. You must trust me, my son." Friar Lawrence sighed heavily. "Though you have no reason to do so."

Romeo struggled. If *he* hadn't died, what about Juliet? Maybe it had all been a terrible dream, and she was alive, and waiting for him. Romeo bolted upright, pushing the friar away.

For the love of God, he saw—

The figure moved out of the shadows, revealing himself. He was tall, dark-haired, and dressed in a long black robe with black mutton sleeves. He wore a black-and-scarlet cap decorated with a gold tassel. His face was long, and pale, and his eyes glowed crimson. And his *teeth* were long, and sharp, and pointed at the ends, like daggers.

"*Vampiro*," Romeo whispered, crossing himself. He knew of such things—damned creatures, shunned by God, attacking the living and ripping out their throats. Unholy.

To his shock, the creature hissed and took a step back. Romeo lifted his hand weakly, making a cross with his thumb and fist.

"Romeo, you know me as your father confessor," Friar Lawrence told him, holding him tightly, demanding his attention. "But I dabble in other matters. Matters of magic, and sorcery."

"W-what evil is this?" Romeo managed, staring at the silhouette of the vampire. "What of my love?"

"Listen carefully, and make no sound," the friar said again. "My plan went awry. I gave Juliet a draught of poison that gave her the mien of death, and sent you a message telling you to rescue her inside the crypt of Capulet."

"I received no such letter!" Romeo cried.

"That letter, alas, never reached you. When you found her, to all appearances dead—you took a poison. If you'd drank any more of it, it would have killed you. As it was, your flesh cooled with the slowing of your heart, and your parents' physician declared that you had expired. Next *she* awoke, believed you dead, and stabbed herself through the heart. And that, alas, did send her to the angels."

Romeo grabbed the friar's hand. "Then kill me, Father. Feed me to that monster so I might hasten to catch up with her!"

"Hush, listen," Friar Lawrence said fiercely. "*You* would have been a different matter, easy to revive, save that before I could intervene they spirited your body away and put you in the earth. They had no way of knowing that they had buried you alive."

"God's blood!" Romeo cried in horror. "And I thought I was being punished."

"The ordeal was too much for you. You were near death when I found you." He paused. "Too near."

"But Juliet *is* dead," Romeo groaned, gripping the man's hand more tightly.

"Hsst, man. Attend me." The priest peered into his eyes. "Recall that I told you I know of matters magic."

Romeo crossed himself again. "Of sorcery?" He dropped his hands to his side. "What care I then, if you have appealed to the devil himself? If there is hope, then tell me. If not, let me die."

"There is," Friar Lawrence confirmed. "The soul of Juliet is under an enchantment now, and by my charge, she will find her way back to you, and only you—if you are alive to welcome her. To love her."

"Then let me make haste to find her," Romeo ordered the friar, swinging his legs over the side of what he now realized was the friar's homely cot. He was in Friar Lawrence's cell, beneath his rows of books and bottles of herbals.

The old man lowered his head. "It is not so simple as that. I have committed many sins in this, my son. I usurped Juliet's father's authority and performed the holy rite to wed her to her mortal enemy. I thought I could succeed in forcing peace in Verona, when even our prince had failed. And I arranged false death for her, which came to true death in the end.

"The poison and your untimely burial claimed your life, Romeo. This is the worst of my sins: I have done a thing to make you come back. But not as you were." He raised a hand, and the vampire stepped forward, holding a simple brass goblet. Steam rose into the chill air.

Romeo stared at it, bewildered.

"Drink, and live," the vampire said to him as he drew near, and held the goblet out. There was a deep gash in the vampire's wrist.

The coppery scent of dark blood wafted toward him. Romeo licked his lips, horrified, aware that he wanted it with all his slowing heart. Needed it.

"What have you done?" Romeo demanded.

"All that I could. And so must you," Friar Lawrence said. "For Juliet."

"For Juliet," Romeo rasped, as the vampire gave him the cup.

He parted his lips, and his world shattered.

Verona, the Present

How much blood have I drunk since then? How many spells have I attempted, how many prayers have I uttered, in my endless waiting? How much pain have I caused?

In his villa, Romeo gazed out at the gardens for a moment. Lavender, roses, orange-tree flowers, and lilies. He knew that the rosy pull of dawn splashed against the plaster and stone walls, and he must go into his coffin and rest. The preparations to celebrate Juliet's transformation would continue—the villa scrubbed from top to bottom by dozens of servants; her coffin elaborately carved. Rose petals would cover the satin shrouds his love would lay in before she lived forever.

I have found her. She's mine again.

She hadn't yet answered his text. The little fear snaked its way into his mind once more. The fear of losing her again was as consuming as the fear that he had lost her forever.

His boots rang on the marble as he turned a corner and walked down the hall toward Juliet's bedroom. The little maid was using a carpet sweeper on the runner—he hated the grinding cacophony of modern vacuum cleaners. She was the one with the scars on her face, and the limp. He couldn't remember her name, nor what kind of accident had ruined her so badly. She was of no importance, except that she stood between him and his Juliet. She hurried to move aside as he passed by.

He reached Juliet's room and rapped expectantly on the door. His hearing was excellent: on the other side of the door, Juliet's heartbeat quickened.

He took that for an invitation and opened the door.

Claire Johnson, his Juliet, was seated before the ornately engraved mirror of entwined cupid's arrows and roses, listening to her iPod and typing on the laptop he'd bought for her. Of course she wasn't sending out any email; that was forbidden. She was here in secret, and must so remain. To that, she had enthusiastically agreed.

His gaze lingered on her, even while the hideous noise from her iPod jangled his nerves. She was wearing the white linen nightgown he had ordered for her from Padua over a pair of ripped black leggings and a purple tank top. She was barefoot. He felt a small disappointment. Not at all ladylike. Somehow, given the closeness of the hour, he had thought she might take more pains with her appearance.

Her blue-streaked hair had grown out more slowly than he'd wished—it had been as short as his was now when she arrived—and it only curled around her ears. That would be its length, then; the Change would make her changeless. She'd taken out her piercings in her eyebrow and her nose—so barbaric!—and had stopped painting her fingernails black.

Romeo had taken her on nighttime tours of Verona, and descended with her into the Capulets' tomb. There she had seen the bones and dust of a thousand years of Capulets. He had shown her the oil portrait of Juliet herself, and Claire had grown dizzy and pale, and fallen to her knees.

"It *is* me," she'd whispered. "I'm Juliet."

He had expected the shock to restore her memory—that she would be "more" Juliet than she was now. Perhaps in time.

She would have eternity to remember.

Claire-Juliet looked up from the dressing table. Of course she couldn't see his reflection—he no longer had one—but when she half-turned and saw him standing in the doorway, color rose in her cheeks and she pulled the earbuds out. They dangled around her neck and rested against the delicious pulse of her vein. She closed the laptop lid and rested her hands on it.

He put his arms around her, gazing down with rapture. "I texted you."

"Oh." She hesitated. "I can't find my phone."

"Careless girl," he said lightly. "Again? I'll buy another. Twenty. When I awake tomorrow evening, I will rise as a bridegroom. And you, Juliet, will live—and love—forever with me."

"Right," she said again, and smiled briefly. Her heart was thundering.

"I know you're nervous," he said. "But you won't feel the things I felt. I'll give you the painkillers first." But not the tetrodox. It was too strong. He remembered his anger, that someone had tampered with the old man. His promise to punish the transgressor. "It will be over so fast!"

"Cool," she said. She reached up on tiptoe and kissed him hard. She was trembling. He could feel his fangs beginning to lengthen and took a courtly step away. She came toward him; he eased her gently out of reach.

"I love thee," he whispered.

"Awesome," she replied, her voice cracking.

The poisoning's culprit had not yet been found, and Romeo felt his good humor sink with the moon. Love for Juliet had softened his mood, but now, as he remembered the foul taste and compared it with Lucenzo's good blood, he felt himself grow angry once more. He told Lucenzo to keep looking, surveyed the preparations, and yelled at the staff for not hanging the festoons properly.

Then Romeo went down into the little tomb Lucenzo's grandfather had helped him design—Lucenzo was mortal, and his family had served Romeo for centuries. Romeo had not bestowed the gift of vampirism on any of Lucenzo's ancestors—in part because they had not wanted it—but Romeo knew Lucenzo had hopes.

Romeo pushed back the lid of the stone sarcophagus. He sank into the coffin layered with earth from the church-yard of seven hundred years before. Weariness washed over him, and he crossed his hands over his chest—most com-fortable for sleeping—and closed his eyes. The preparations for Juliet's initiation into vampirism would continue in the daylight while he slept.

The sun leeched his strength and he began to doze. When vampires slept, they had no sense of the passage of time. That was one of the first things his vampiric maker, Scarlatti, had taught him. The noble bloodsucker had trained him in many things—how to hunt, what could kill him, how to pass among humans as mortal. Then Scarlatti had met the True Death at Romeo's hands. The older vampire took too many chances, hunting too closely to Verona. *Self-defense*, Romeo had told himself. Friar Lawrence had been shocked to his core that Romeo could so easily kill the vampire who had given him life.

C⁓

Verona, 1372

"Your blood is cold," Friar Lawrence had whispered. He was very old by then, doddering, and forgetful.

"My blood is dead," Romeo retorted.

"I did not foresee this. I thought you would remain the gold-hearted youth that you were."

Romeo drew himself up. "And so I have. Look in any mirror." He lips curled in cruelty. "Ah, but I have no reflection. I am as you would have me made."

The friar raised a palsied hand. "To help you."

"To torment me."

"She will come," Friar Lawrence promised.

But as the years passed, and Juliet didn't arrive, Romeo's dead blood grew icy. He gathered up Friar Lawrence's books and threw them in the river. Tore the old man's cell apart and burned the bed and his study desk in a bonfire. He went on a rampage, slaughtering innocents even when he didn't need blood.

"You have become a monster," Friar Lawrence had told him, cowering from him.

"Then give me what I want!" Romeo had shouted at him. "If you be a man of magic, bring her to me!"

Friar Lawrence shook his head. "You must have patience."

"I must have Juliet!"

Romeo struck the friar, forgetting that his unnatural strength was twice that of a man. Friar Lawrence sprawled on the stone floor of his cell. Hard-hearted, Romeo made no move to help him up. Instead, he turned his back and disappeared into the shadows.

Friar Lawrence had written him a letter that night, which Romeo found after the old man had died:

Romeo,

This is the last letter I shall write in this world, and I address it to you. You were such a good youth, a chivalrous gentleman, but you have become a heartless knave. Your love for Juliet has driven you mad. I urge you to repent. Perhaps it is God's will that you should let her go.

Friar Lawrence

After Friar Lawrence's death, Romeo's fury scourged the countryside like a force of nature. The sorcerer was gone, and with his magic, and Romeo was alone. Let Juliet go? Never.

Sorrow and anger festered inside him, burning away his humanity. He became meaner, crueler. He outlived generations of Capulets and Montagues, hating them all, because none of them were Juliet.

And then . . . Claire.

Romeo smiled in his sleep, his fangs glistening.

Verona, the Present

He awoke with the rising of the moon and pushed back his coffin lid. Nearly delirious with joy, he climbed the stairs. He was shaking like the eager youth beneath his true love's balcony.

The time had come.

He unlocked the heavy steel door separating his crypt from the rest of the villa. His servants were shouting and running everywhere. Lucenzo turned, spotted him, and hurried over. His face was as pale as ash.

"She's gone," Lucenzo said. When Romeo didn't seem to understand, he added, "Clara. Giulietta." He was clearly stressed, using the Italian version of her name.

"*What?*"

Romeo pushed past Lucenzo and raced to Juliet's room. The drawers of her dresser were open, the bed rumpled. Her laptop lay on top of the pillow.

"She took nothing but what she brought," Lucenzo said, "and . . . money. She took money."

Romeo tore through the room. The gauze gown was there. The ripped leggings, not. The iPod, gone. He was dizzy. He could barely think.

Then he picked up the laptop and opened the lid. Plopping onto the bed, he typed in her password—*Juliet*—and waited for her mail to open.

There was a letter for him:

Dear Romeo,

I'm gone. Please don't try to find me. Please just let me go.

I wanted to believe that I'm your Juliet, but I know I'm not. I don't know why I have the birthmark and stuff but I just can't go through with it. I tried to be how you wanted but it's just too scary. You're too scary. I tried to tell you but I

*knew you wouldn't listen. For a while I thought
you were just eccentric, you know, some rich
crazy Italian guy, but . . . you're real.*

*I met this guy. We're together now so please
just leave me alone.*

I hope you find your Juliet.

Claire

"No!" Romeo roared. He hurled the laptop at the wall;
Lucenzo dove, grabbing it like a soccer ball and skidding
across the stone floor. "Find her! Find them both! Drag them
back here!"

His servants scattered, both to obey his orders and to stay
out of his way. Romeo tore the sheets off the bed. Ripped
the pillows to shreds. Whirled around and pushed over the
dressing table. Wood shattered and cracked. Glass shattered.
He pounded the wall. Plaster fell in clumps. Then, he fell to
the floor and sobbed.

Then he grabbed his cell phone and called her. It went
to voice.

"Juliet," he whispered. "Come back."

Someone was standing in the doorway. Looking up
sharply, he saw a flash of movement and darted with blinding speed across the threshold.

It was the ugly little maid, retreating as fast as she possibly could.

"Stop," he ordered her.

She obeyed. She was no taller than his shoulders; she
was wearing a white blouse and black trousers, the uniform
of his servants, and black athletic shoes.

"Turn around."

Her black hair hung around her face as if she were trying to conceal the scars that zigzagged across her cheeks. Her mouth was twisted to one side, and her nose was too big. Her eyes were chocolate brown, quite deep-set.

"What do you know of this?" he demanded.

"Nothing, *signor*," she said.

Before her gaze shifted to the floor, she glanced at him with obvious pity. He was incensed. Who was *she* to pity *him*?

"Then go away, *donna brutta*," he sneered at her. *Ugly woman.*

She flinched and did as he asked. Lucenzo approached, skirting around the maid as if she weren't there. He was waving a little notebook.

The maid disappeared down the hall.

"She got into a blue Fiat Panda with a young man," Lucenzo announced. "He pulled over and she got out. He had to talk her back into the car. A boy walking a dog saw the whole thing."

Romeo took that in. "And?"

"We're looking, *signor*," Lucenzo said, sounding less enthusiastic than when he had been waving the notebook.

"*You didn't find them?*"

"They had a head start." Lucenzo licked his lips. "I've sent cars after them, sir. Motorcycles."

"Get out there and look yourself! Or don't come back!" Romeo's face changed. His fangs lengthened and he hissed at the man. He heard Lucenzo's heartbeat pick up and a sadistic thrill rushed through him. *Be afraid*, he said. *Be afraid for your life, if you don't come back with her.*

"Sir," Lucenzo ventured, "if she's *not* Juliet, then why—"

"Because she is!" Romeo shouted. To his horror, he burst into tears again. "She *is*!"

He called, left messages. Texted. *Where are you? Come back!* Seven hundred years! Seven centuries! God could not be so cruel. Or maybe He was. Maybe this was Romeo's punishment for trying to kill himself. God dangled hope in front of him, snatched it away.

"Then I defy you, stars," he ground out, stumbling into the garden, pulling over statues, knocking over stone benches; ripping out vines, flowers, ferns. He was destroying his home. His sanctuary.

His holding pen.

All night he ranted, raved, demolishing anything he could lay his hands on. He destroyed the music room, where her transformation was to have taken place. A bit of drugged wine, and draining her nearly to death. Then giving her his own blood to drink. Then forever, together, eternally young.

Now . . . nothing.

He called her again. Again. The villa was quiet. The servants were hiding. The sun pulled on him as it began to rise, burning him from the inside out. It hurt, and made him clumsy. He slammed inside the protective walls like a man on the verge of losing his sight.

Three hours later, a text message came in on his cell phone.

Help.

It was from her phone. Then his phone rang, and wild with joy, he connected.

"We've found them," Lucenzo said through the speaker.

"Is she all right?"

"She's afraid."

He frowned. "Of . . . ?"

"Of you, Romeo."

Romeo flinched. How could that be? Afraid of him? Of *him?*

"Sir?" Lucenzo said.

"Bring them here." Romeo's voice was hoarse. The sun was about to spread its rays across the horizon. "Keep them until I rise."

"Keep them . . . "

He paused. "Safe," Romeo said.

Hurting, he lay down in the earth.

Vampires lose track of time when they're asleep, and they don't dream. But that day, Romeo dreamed that he was holding Juliet. They were very old, and they sat before a fireplace surrounded by their children and grandchildren. Juliet was showing them love letters they had written to each other, smiling at Romeo with so much love as she picked up stack after stack. Some were written on parchment. Others, on modern-day, heavy stationery the color of cream. All these hundreds of years, she had written him letters, not knowing where to send them. And now they were his.

When Romeo woke with the night, he charged out of his coffin and raced up the stairs. He remembered his dream about the letters, and it gave him hope.

"She's here," Lucenzo said, keeping a cautious distance as Romeo burst across the threshold of the crypt staircase. "Please, sir, she's terrified."

Romeo nodded. "And the man?"

"We have him, too. He's the son of the head gardener."

"I hope *Signor* Gardener has more than one son," Romeo declared, as his fangs lengthened and he allowed the blood-lust to come over him. "Where are they?"

"In the music room," Lucenzo told him.

Lucenzo trailed behind him as he walked to the room. The white columns of the room were still tipped over, and their festoons of white ribbons and roses wafted in shredded tatters, intermixed with the rose petals scattered on the hardwood floor. A harp stood in the center of the room, and beside it, Claire—Juliet—was on the floor, crying and clinging to a young man Romeo had never seen. The young man had blond hair pulled into a ponytail, and blue eyes that darted nervously back and forth as the lord of the manor planted his feet in front of both of them.

"Please," she managed to croak out, "please don't hurt us. Just let us go."

"Why should I?" he demanded.

"Because she's not Juliet!" the blond man yelled at him. Then, as if he realized how foolish it was to shout at Romeo, he lowered his voice. "She's not . . . Juliet."

Romeo watched them holding each other, weeping, and he trembled. She was *his*.

"You just don't remember," he began. It occurred to him that the son of the gardener knew too much to be left alive. He was glad. "But I *know* you are Juliet, Claire."

Deep sobs made her shoulders jerk. She shook her head violently.

"I knew a long time ago that I wasn't. But I . . . I had nowhere else to go. I'm sorry. I thought I could fake it but, it's just too . . . *gross*."

He frowned at her. "Then why did you text me for help?"

She raised swollen eyes toward him. "I didn't. I told you, I lost my phone."

"Then who is this?" he asked, showing her the message.

"I don't know."

"You have to let us go," the man insisted. "We've done nothing to you."

Nothing but rip out my unbeating heart.

"Everyone here is loyal to me," Romeo said. "They would rather die than reveal my secrets. If your father works for me, then he's made the same vow." He gave Lucenzo a look. Lucenzo flushed at this lapse in security.

"I don't know this young man," Lucenzo declared.

"I came for a visit, from university," the young man said. "And I saw her at the balcony . . ."

Romeo's body contracted as if he had been stabbed through the heart. Claire—no, Juliet, she *was* Juliet!—gave him a look that reminded him of the scarred maid. He raised the hand in which he held the cell phone, clenching it so tightly it began to crack, and she cowered, sobbing.

"I'm sorry," she said. "I really am. But I'm not her. I'm not."

"Let me take them away," Lucenzo said. "Don't do anything you might regret. Perhaps in time . . ."

It was in his heart to refuse. To kill the boy who had confused her. To drain him in front of her, make her sorry . . . to make her shriek . . .

God, I have become a monster.

He was overcome with anger and grief, shame and despair. Friar Lawrence was right. He should have died, rather than become this. How could Juliet love him? Was there anything of Romeo left to love?

"Get them out of here. Everyone," Romeo said without looking at him. "All the servants. Every single one."

Lucenzo hesitated. "Sir?"

"Get them out!" Romeo bellowed. "Now!"

For two or three more seconds, Lucenzo stayed. Then he turned and walked away. Romeo kept his head lowered as he listened to the heartbeats of each person in the villa. They grew fainter in clumps; then in smaller groups; and then there was one left, lingering, as if hoping to be called back.

Then that one left, too.

He sank to his knees and bowed his head. He was done. Awash in misery, and self-hatred. How could he have thought this would be what she wanted? How could he ever have hoped?

"Madness," he whispered.

Nothing tired vampires except the rising sun, and Romeo felt its pull as he got to his feet. Despairing, he surveyed the destruction of the music room, which he barely remembered having caused. He trudged out, numb with sorrow, and staggered through the villa.

Down to his coffin? Was there any reason to preserve his own life? He was at the end. All of it had been for nothing. Juliet was not coming.

She was never coming.

Then he paused, detecting the weak beating of one more heart. Lucenzo? Or—

"Juliet?" he cried, unable to stop himself. "Claire?"

There was no answer but the heartbeat, and he realized it was coming from outside—in his gardens. The scene of the crime of the gardener's son. He remembered Lucenzo telling him that Claire had gotten out of the car, and the boy—Romeo didn't even know his name—had talked her into getting back in.

"Claire?"

The sun was threatening to rise, but he had to know who was there.

The heartbeat pumped against his eardrums like the clang of a distant buoy. He cast off through the shambles of his once-exquisite garden—across wrenched fields of orange-tree flowers and lilies, listening as the heartbeat grew.

There, beneath a toppled Grecian column! It was strongest there, although it was very weak. It was the heartbeat of a dying person.

He rushed toward the white cylinder. Black athletic shoes stuck out from beneath it. He made his way around to the other end, moving as through mud. The sun was rising. He should go back.

The column had fallen at an angle, just missing the head of the horribly scarred little maid. Claire's cell phone lay in her outstretched hand.

As he approached, her eyes fluttered open. For a moment they were blank, and then they focused on his face. A strange, strangled cry bubbled out of her mouth, along with a trickle of blood.

"Romeo," she whispered, and then he knew.

It was she.

"Oh, God, oh, my God," he cried. "Juliet."

Juliet.

Juliet.

Juliet.

He fell to his knees and covered her disfigured face with kisses. Gray light glowed against the scars. Sunlight.

Juliet.

Juliet.

Juliet.

More blood trickled from her mouth.

"You texted me for help?"

"You came," she whispered brokenly.

"Why didn't you tell me who you were?" he cried. But he knew why: he had become a demon, a heartless fiend. Evil.

"Ugly," she whispered, echoing his thoughts.

"I, yes, I have become ugly." He wrapped his arms around the column, grunting as he yanked and pulled. It was too heavy. He couldn't budge it, not when he was so weak. It was crushing the life out of her, as the sun was smothering the life out of him. His back began to smoke. He felt prickles of heat along the nape of his neck, his scalp. It was too near day. "I have become a monster, hopeless, loveless."

"No. I am ugly," she said.

"Oh, Juliet, is that why you hid from me?" he wailed as he dug in his heels and pushed against the cold, unforgiving stone. "Only that?"

"Hie hence, be gone," she murmured. "More light and light it grows."

"I have more care to stay than will to go," he replied, fighting back tears.

He stared at the blood on her lips. It would replenish him. Then he would be able to push the column off her, carry her into the house, and transform her. They would be together, at last. If he had time, only a little more time . . .

"Ah," he moaned, as the pain washed over him. Then he realized: "You drugged the old man. To stop me."

"Sì." Her heartbeat slowed even more, barely beating. She was on the verge of death. And he, as well, for the sun was about to break through the last vestiges of the night.

He was flooded with remorse. "I thought she was you. Did I betray you, love?"

"I almost lost you," she whispered.

"Never. You would never lose me." He choked back a sob, clenching his teeth as the lassitude, so like death, gripped his limbs.

"I wrote you letters," she said. "I have them all."

"I will read them," he promised her. He realized that had been the message of his dream, and tears streamed down his face.

"In heaven," she said faintly.

He bowed his head. "This is my doing, all of it. I was too blind, too rash. If only I had seen that *I* was to come to *you* . . . that you were here."

"I am here," she echoed. And she gazed at him with the love he had waited for, for seven hundred years. Did she smile with that twisted mouth? Or was she squinting against the sun's glare?

"My love . . . as boundless . . ."

"Lovely. Beauty too rich for use, for earth too dear," he serenaded her.

". . . as the sea."

"Oh, my love, my wife." He tried to hold her, and to comfort her. The sun had fully risen. He was out of time. He was timeless.

"Thus, with a kiss, I die." He pressed his lips to hers, forever.

Which happened first, her death, or his? As he burned in the blazing sun, gazing down at that dear, beautiful, ruined face, Romeo dreamed that they died at the same instant; and that because of her goodness, her faithfulness, and her love, he went to heaven with her. Whoever it was said that vampires did not dream, was a liar.

And for those who believe that true love never dies . . . they live in a state of grace, from one century of dreams to the next.

The Other Side

HEATHER BREWER

Blinding pain ripped through Tarrah's shoulder and she wrenched away from it, snapping from sleep and shuffling off her disturbing dreams like she would a too-heavy blanket. She opened her eyes, but was no better off for having done so—the room was pitch-dark as night, its blackness weighing down on every inch of space that surrounded her. But that wasn't the strangest part of what had woken her; not by a long shot. She was on her side, her hands bound behind her, something cold and metal linking her wrists— handcuffs, she was almost certain.

The floor felt like concrete. It was some kind of stone, so cold and hard that her skin burned against it painfully. She couldn't help but wonder how long someone would have to lie on cold concrete to make their skin feel like it was on fire, but imagined it would take a few hours, at minimum. And judging by the rumbling of her stomach, it had been at least that long. Stretching out her shivering fingers, which were all but numb from being bound for who knows how long, she brushed their tips against more metal—a cylinder, like a pipe or pole. The cuffs attached her to it. She was tied up, trapped, in a dark place, and had no memory whatsoever of how she'd gotten here. Terror painted her insides, but she forced herself to remain calm. Her hands slid along the pole, feeling, hoping that she'd be able to either yank or lift her way free, but her explorations found nothing but metal . . . that is, until they met with flesh.

Someone else's flesh.

Hands, cool and still, also ringed with handcuffs, also attached to the pipe. Tarrah jolted at the touch. The hands were larger than hers, masculine. Her thoughts skidded to a halt. Now there wasn't just the mystery of how she got here to solve; there was also this.

She wondered briefly if the man she was attached to was dead. He might be, and if he was, who had killed him? Shaking, Tarrah turned her head, scraping her cheek on the concrete as she tried impossibly to get a look at her fellow prisoner in the darkness. She squinted her eyes, wanting to get a good look but hoping to block out any gore—if there was any gore. If he was a corpse, she didn't really want to see. She didn't *want* to see him anyway, she *had* to see him, had to know if she was lying in a cold, strange room handcuffed to a pole with a dead guy.

But she could just barely make out his silhouette in the darkness.

Parting her now trembling lips, amazed by the aching dryness of her mouth, Tarrah whispered into the air, hoping like crazy that he'd respond, even with something as insignificant as a grunt. Anything at all that indicated life. "Hey . . ."

Her voice seemed horribly foreign and somehow wrong in the blank emptiness of the room, but she had to speak. It was the only way to reach the man she was handcuffed to, the only way to check his pulse without touching him again. He was cold. Cold like death. Or was he simply chilled from spending time on the freezing concrete floor? It felt like the air-conditioning was on, but there was no breeze from any vent. It was almost like being inside a cooler.

"Hello?" Her whisper sounded empty, hollow in the night air. Night. Was it night? Or were they locked in a cellar, far away from the reaches of sunlight? How long had they been here? And who had put them here? Desperation fueled her cries. "Hey! Wake up!"

Silence was the only reply. And then Tarrah knew that the man attached to her with handcuffs and a metal pole was dead. Images filled her mind. Dark, disturbing images of a bloated stomach and creepy crawly awful things dancing on his tongue. She turned her head away as the tickle of a scream edged up her throat.

"Wh-what's going on? Tarrah?" The man's voice was muffled, as if he were just waking from a heavy sleep. From behind Tarrah came scraping noises, as he struggled his way into wakefulness, possibly moving from one nightmare to the next. Corey. It was Corey. Relief filled her immediately. If she had to be tied up in a strange place, at least it was with her boyfriend. If he still was her boyfriend after the argument they'd shared. She lay quietly, trying to block out the horrible things she'd said to him the last time they saw one another, and allowed him his moment of utter terror, giving him time to accept the reality of their present predicament. There was something comforting about his fear. Just knowing that he was frightened and confused as well settled her heart into a more normal rhythm.

Once he'd stopped struggling, she said, "Oh thank god, Corey. I thought you were some dead guy."

He shifted, maybe to get a little more comfortable, and said, "Why am I naked?"

Tarrah whipped her head around to her boyfriend, who was grinning. He was also completely clothed, as she saw when her eyes finally adjusted to the darkness. She shook her head. Why did he always have to act like that in moments of stress? He had a weird way of easing the tension in any given situation, but she didn't exactly appreciate his brand of humor at the moment. "Don't be a jerk. This is serious. Do you remember how you got here?"

She reached back in her own memories, straining to recall the last thing she'd done before she woke up on this cold floor. After a moment of contemplation, she remembered. She'd just gotten out of the shower and put pajamas on, getting ready for sleep in her usual ritual. She was just brushing her teeth when everything went completely blank. Her memories went dark, as if there were nothing at all to remember between that moment and now.

Corey's breathing was settling now, the panic slipping from it some. Even in the darkness she could see that his false grin was fading fast. "Last thing I remember is sitting on my couch, messing with my Gibson. This one song, by this band The Mopey Teenage Bears, it's a killer. The bridge has been messin' with me for weeks. I just can't seem to nail it. Oh, and I thought about calling you, but when I looked at the clock I realized it was getting pretty late . . ."

Corey's voice had slipped from alarmed and deeply disturbed to one of casual conversation, as if they weren't both tied up and chained in someone's basement. And as if they hadn't gotten into a big fight the last time they'd talked. It sent Tarrah into flights of panic. Her teeth chattered as she shouted, "Stop it, Corey! Stop talking like we're not going to die!"

What other reason would some psycho have to chain them up in this way? If their lives weren't in danger, then just what the hell was going on?

Corey grew quiet then. After a moment, perhaps in an effort to calm her down, he said, "Who says we're going to die?"

Low, metallic laughter pierced the darkness. The kind of laughter that sends chills up your arms and makes the tiny hairs on the back of your neck stand at full attention. Tarrah ignored the voice in her head—the one that screamed for her not to look, not to turn her head toward the frightening, horrible laughter, to squeeze her eyes shut and will it all away—and looked toward the spot she was sure the laughter had come from. All she saw was darkness, but the moment her eyes connected with the spot she knew the voice had generated from, it spoke. "There's no avoiding death. Eventually, it comes to us all."

Tarrah's jaw was shaking from the cold. She peered into the darkness, but still couldn't see anything. If she could just see the creep, she'd feel better in some small way. Hell, if she could see anything, she'd feel at least some small comfort.

"But before you die, you will suffer, I'm afraid, for my needs." The voice was sarcastic and cruel in Tarrah's ears. Then there was a sound. The sound of something being dropped. Light pierced the darkness. The beam of a small flashlight slashed through the black with brilliant white, then tumbled forward, toward Tarrah and Corey, as it rolled away from the faceless speaker across the room. Tarrah's eyes followed the beam, trying desperately to steal glimpses of where they were, so that maybe they could find a way out . . . if they ever got out of the handcuffs, that is.

As the light moved, it bounced this way and that, showing cinderblock walls, not a single window, and the concrete floor that they were already well acquainted with. Then the light's movement slowed, and the beam fell on Tarrah. The faceless voice clucked its tongue, and Tarrah wished very much that she could somehow curl up inside her head, where the voice could not reach. Its tone was oddly complimentary. "My, you are a pretty thing. A shame. Death comes too quick for some. But it always comes, children. No matter how loudly we beg for it not to. And we all do. Money says you will, too."

Behind her, Corey's silence spoke volumes. She hoped that he was horrified for her. For them. Because she was pretty damn horrified herself.

The sadistic chuckle found its way again from the darkness, giving itself form as it bent over to retrieve the fallen flashlight. The man squatted there in front of her, and at first, Tarrah was certain he was ogling her in some perverted way. But then she realized where he was looking. He was focused only on her neck, and nothing below.

Tarrah became fixated on the man's face. His features were shadowed, but she could tell that his jaw was sharp and angular, almost feminine. In any other situation, Tarrah might have given him a second glance. He was handsome, almost pretty. His nose was smooth and straight. And his eyes . . .

Tarrah gasped aloud and drew back—as far back as she could—away from the man, the . . . creature that was now crouching just inches in front of her, leaning in closer with a bemused smirk on its lips.

His—its—eyes were piercing. A shining glint of darkness, even in the pitch-black room. This creature . . . it wasn't right. It wasn't normal, not at all like she and Corey. It was something else entirely.

As if in response to her unspoken thought, the creature leaned in closer and spread its lips into a grin, revealing porcelain teeth that glistened in the low light. Tarrah sat, fascinated and frightened, staring at those teeth, not knowing what to make of them. Just as her mind had settled on a word to describe the beast, the word flitted away again, and she was left only with her racing thoughts sprinting to catch up with her racing heart.

Corey's voice broke the moment. It was eerily calm and collected, as if he were strangely accustomed to defusing situations like this. She had no way of knowing whether he had spied the creature's eyes or teeth before he spoke. "I don't know who you are or what you want, buddy, but if you don't let us go, you're going to regret it. I can promise you that."

Wordlessly, their captor collected the flashlight and stood, and then moved around Tarrah to Corey. Tarrah wrenched around to watch as it withdrew an ear thermometer from its pocket and put the medical tool to Corey's ear—Corey, who had normal teeth and crystalline blue eyes; Corey, who defiantly did not shrink away at the man's touch. After the thermometer beeped, the man—the creature—sighed and said, "That settles it then. You're first."

Tarrah watched the thing closely as it reached for Corey's cuffs. It pressed a finger to the center of Corey's handcuffs and the lock released with a small click, as if the cuffs had been programmed to release only at the monster's touch. Then it pulled Corey roughly up by his arm. Corey didn't fight back. In fact, he looked too exhausted and too damn cold to fight off the creature.

A horrible feeling curled up in the pit of Tarrah's stomach—one that told her something bad was coming, and that this might be the last time she ever saw Corey alive. "What are you doing? Where are you taking him?"

Her last word was cut off by the slamming of the door. She hadn't even realized a door was being opened—there was no light behind it, nothing at all to indicate that a portal to somewhere other than this room had been opened. But when it closed, when that metallic *thunk* had sealed her once more inside, Tarrah felt her insides go soft, as if they'd given up before her fight had even begun.

She was trapped. She was being held in a dark, cold place by a monster. And she had no idea how to escape.

And Corey . . . poor Corey. Who knew what the creature was doing to him now? Torturing him? Drinking his blood? Worse? With those teeth, who knew what the thing was capable of? Devouring Corey? Certainly. Like a monster from a fairy tale. But that was impossible, she knew. Those things existed only on the pages of books or in the flicker of film upon a screen.

Didn't they?

Tarrah pulled at her restraints, but they wouldn't give. After a few deep breaths, she focused on relaxing every muscle in her body. She thought if she relaxed enough and wiggled just so, she might be able to slip from the cuffs. Isn't that what Houdini did? He controlled his breathing, relaxed his muscles, and *voilà*! He was free of his binds. She'd read about it in some book Corey had given her a few years ago. But after fifteen minutes or so of relaxing, and then wriggling, pulling, cursing, and trying desperately not to scream, Tarrah realized that Houdini she was not. A tear slid down her cheek to the floor below, and Tarrah flew into panic, flailing against the cuffs in a desperate attempt to break free. Her panic gave way to sobs, and after a while, her throat felt raw and hollow.

The unseen door opened again after what felt like about a half hour and Tarrah almost gasped at the brief glow of the flashlight as it entered the room. Once the door closed, her eyes adjusted to the darkness again and she watched as the nameless monster dropped Corey to the floor. Corey went down like a stone, and barely made a sound. Tarrah had her eyes locked on her boyfriend, who looked so tired, so weak, that she could barely stand to think about what might have transpired behind that door. Had the creature fed on him? Drained him almost to the point of death? And if it had . . . why had it returned Corey to this room without finishing him off? Were they being kept for some other purpose, or more of the same?

Tarrah flicked her eyes to Corey, who moaned and sluggishly moved about, barely conscious. It had to be due to loss of blood. "What did you do to him, you monster?"

The creature moved over to where Tarrah lay shivering and put a thermometer to her ear. Her heart thumped loudly in her chest. It was her turn now, her turn to see what was on the other side of that door, to learn what sadistic purpose the monster was keeping them for. The beast pushed the button, and she heard a small beep. After checking her temperature, it nodded thoughtfully. "It won't be long now, girl. I'll be back for you in an hour or so. I suggest you say your good-byes before I return."

Tarrah clamped her mouth shut, refusing to speak. Talking to her captor wouldn't do them any good. The monster wouldn't listen, and after seeing what it had done to Corey, she knew nothing she could say would ever convince it to let them go.

Capping the thermometer, the beast wordlessly stood and slipped back out of the unseen door. Tarrah looked over at her unconscious boyfriend. She wanted her voice to sound confident and calm, but what came out was more like a panicked squeak. "Corey?"

But Corey wasn't moving, and as far as she could tell, he wasn't breathing either. Panic enveloped her again, welling up from deep within, and she stretched her leg outward, trying desperately to reach Corey so that she could nudge him into wakefulness, back into life. As she stretched, it seemed that time slowed and she could see into the future. A future without Corey. A future where she'd never apologized for pushing him away last weekend. A future that lasted only minutes before the monster returned to kill her as well. Just as her foot was within reach of Corey's leg, she hesitated. What if she touched him and discovered that he really was dead? If she didn't touch him at all, could she go on pretending that he was fine and that they were going to get out of this mess somehow?

But there was no turning back. She couldn't live with a lie. She had to know the truth, had to know if her boyfriend was okay. She pointed her toe and nudged his still form. "Corey? Come on, answer me. Are you okay? You have to be okay. Please say something."

At first, Corey didn't move. But then, ever so slowly, he groaned and strained to lift his head. When he met her eyes, she released a burdened, relieved sigh and had to hold in a gasp at the sight of his eyes—her favorite part of him. Crystalline blue and beautiful, even in the darkness of this horrible place. In her terror, she'd almost forgotten what a looker he was. He gazed at her, sadness flicking across his face, and pulled one corner of his mouth up in a small tug, as if he were trying desperately to retain his sense of optimistic humor. "I guess that depends on your definition of okay. I'm really weak, that's for sure. Dizzy as hell, kinda nauseous. And my neck is really sore. What about you, babe? Are you okay?"

The truth was, Tarrah had never been so not-okay in her entire life. But she couldn't say that or she'd start crying— she could already feel the tears welling up in her throat. So instead, she said, "I thought you were dead."

Corey's voice dropped to a terrified whisper. "That makes two of us, babe."

She bit her bottom lip. Tarrah had never liked it when he called her babe. It seemed so caveman, so possessive and demeaning. But at the moment, it was sweet, so sweet that she was having a hard time keeping the tears at bay. She loved him so much. There had to be a way out of this for both of them.

Recalling what he'd said about hurting, she replied, "What's wrong with your neck? What did it do to you?"

Corey swallowed hard, his eyes dropping in what looked like embarrassment. When he turned his head, she could make out two small holes on the left side of his throat. A horrified gasp escaped her, and a frightened shiver crawled up her spine with the realization that the creature was coming back in an hour to do the same to her. And who knew how long it would continue using them like this? It could keep them here for weeks, she bet. She wretched, her body filling with disgust at the thought. By the time she regained her composure, Corey was looking at her again. He looked wounded, but not defeated. "Tarrah," he said, his tone almost stern, "you have to get out of here before it hurts you. Or worse. You know that, right? You know if you don't escape, it'll kill you, too. Right? I'm as good as dead."

"Don't say that!"

His eyes said it all. He couldn't tell her the horrors he'd faced in the other room, but those horrors had involved pain and blood and he didn't want her to be subjected to them at any cost. She nodded, sniffling away her tears, frightened but touched that he wanted to protect her. The last time they had seen each other, she'd told him she needed some space, that she was thinking about seeing other people. Now she realized that she only said that out of some twisted need for attention. She loved Corey, even if he could be obnoxious sometimes. They'd been together for a long time and she couldn't imagine life without him. Especially now, when faced with the very real possibility of just that. Her words left her mouth in a strangled whisper. "We're getting out of here together. Don't even think about pulling that noble sacrifice routine. I'm finding a way out and taking you with me."

They both went quiet then and neither spoke for several minutes. Tarrah ran a finger along her cuffs, inching her way over the metal, hoping to learn more about it. The material wasn't traditional steel, that was for sure, and the lock seemed to be some sort of fingerprint recognition device. Both meant bad news: that only their captor was capable of freeing them from their binds. She hadn't been able to escape the cuffs, but maybe they would be easier for someone else to snap from a different angle. And the creature had left Corey's hands free. "Do you think you can break my cuffs?" she asked him.

Corey started to crawl over, but stopped, shaking his head. He looked gray, even in the darkness. "I feel so dizzy. Hold on. This might take a minute."

After a few moments, he started to move again. He crawled behind her and got a good look at the cuffs. He pulled hard on the chain that linked her hands, pinching her skin sharply. Her wrist instantly felt wet, which meant she was bleeding. "Ow! Dammit, Corey!"

"Sorry. If I had some tools, this wouldn't be a problem. Man . . . what I'd give for some bolt cutters right now." He sighed heavily. "There is one thing we could try, but I don't know if it's a good idea, Tarrah."

Wrenching her neck around, she met her boyfriend's worried eyes. "What is it? At this point I'm willing to try any-thing. We have to get out of here, right? So what is it?"

Corey's face went pale. He collapsed to the ground, his body trembling.

"Corey!" Tarrah's heart raced. The blood loss, the stress, dragging himself across the room to try to help her get loose. It must have been too much for Corey. He couldn't handle it.

His eyes fluttered for a moment, as if he were on the verge of losing consciousness. Then he stretched his fingers out and laced them with hers. His fingers were warm, so warm that they were almost hot to the touch. His skin burned feverishly. Her fingers shook against his. He was sick, maybe dying, and she had no idea how to get him out of here. And she was the only one who could save him, save them both. Suddenly, the room seemed very large, overwhelming. Corey gave her fingers a weak squeeze and whispered, "I love you, Tarrah."

Large, round tears escaped her eyes and rolled down her cheek to the concrete floor. Instantly, she hated him. Because he was saying good-bye. He was letting go before they even knew things were hopeless. She couldn't let that happen, couldn't say good-bye when there was still a chance they could get free. But her hatred was fleeting. She swallowed her tears, pushing her fear way down deep inside, and whispered, "I love you, too, Corey."

His eyelids fluttered closed and a new terror swept through her. The sound of his labored breathing eased it some: Corey wasn't dead—not yet, anyway. But they didn't have long until he was.

There was nothing she could do. Nothing. She had no tools, none of the strength required to get free. Just her unbound legs and her ungagged mouth. So unless kicking and biting her way free were an option, she was screwed. Of course, when the monster returned and undid her cuffs, fighting wasn't out of the realm of possibility. But she was cold, and the coldness had weakened her so much. No, feet and teeth weren't going to get her out of this. What she needed was to get out of these cuffs and somehow get Corey to safety. She slipped her hand from his and twisted around to see if she'd missed anything, anything at all in the room that might help her. The cut on her wrist burned, so she eased up on it and swept the dark room with her eyes, finding nothing at all but Corey and the pole she was attached to.

Then an idea sparked in her mind.

Tarrah pulled hard on her left arm, until the handcuff dug sharply into the small cut on her wrist. She bit her bottom lip against the pain, trying hard to keep her screams contained within her. The metal tore her skin open further and blood oozed from the wound until her hand and wrist were slick. Slick enough to act as a lubricant. She had to move quickly, or else the blood would dry and she'd have to open the cut again.

She pulled hard, a pained cry escaping her throat, but her action proved fruitful. Blood poured from her wound. Plenty enough to make her wrist slippery. Then she brought her fingers together and pulled again. Her hand slipped free.

She couldn't look at it, couldn't stand to see the mangled gore that was her wrist. Her wound throbbed painfully, but Tarrah counted her blessings. It would have hurt a lot more if she hadn't been seminumbed by the cold. The cuff was still attached to her right hand, but it didn't matter. She was free.

She crawled over to Corey and checked his pulse. He was still alive, but fading fast. All she had to do now was locate the door and hope to hell the stupid thing wasn't locked.

The door swung open, and this time, a blinding light shone from within. The beast's silhouette filled its frame. "Well, well. What do we have here? Resourceful little thing, aren't you?"

She froze. Her mind went completely blank—she had no idea what to do or how to stop what had happened to Corey from happening to her.

It moved closer, clucking its tongue. It sounded vaguely amused. "What did you do? Wriggle yourself free like some kind of animal? Chew off your arm like a trapped coyote, perhaps?"

Tarrah shrank back, but the thing stretched its hand forward and examined her wrist. It shook its head in disapproval. "All that wasted blood. A shame."

The creature reached for her then, as if to pick her up and carry her off to who knows where, and Tarrah found her fight once more, despite the cold's slowing effect on her muscles. She shoved the beast as hard as she could, and once it had stumbled a few feet from her, she kicked, aiming for the most unpleasant target she could imagine. With a growl, it grabbed her—despite the pain, despite her struggles—and lifted her over its shoulder, shushing her like a child. "There now. Calm yourself. Soon it'll all be over and you'll join your boyfriend there in eternity."

A shock of cold surprise bolted through her and she whipped her eyes to Corey. Corey, who lay too still. Corey, whose eyes stared blankly open and unseeing. Her tears let loose and she screamed, pounding on the man's back with balled-up, bloody fists. "He's not dead! He's alive! Corey's alive!"

But even as she screamed the words, she knew them to be untrue. Corey, sweet Corey, the boy she'd loved for so long, the boy who'd drawn Band-Aids all over her cast when she broke her arm, the boy who brought her roses before every date and lilies on every anniversary.

He was dead.

And the monster carrying her had killed him.

She clawed at its neck, and as she wriggled from its grasp, she bit into its forearm. The beast howled and gripped her tighter, dragging her from the dark cellar where Corey lay into the bright room next to it. It slammed her onto what looked and felt like a hospital gurney, knocking the wind from her lungs and the voice from her throat, and strapped her arms down tight. In the bright white of the room—white walls, white sheets—the blood on her wrist seemed almost too red, too real. The creature fastened a thick strap across her chest. There was no moving now, no getting away. Not if that *thing* had anything to say about it.

Tarrah looked around quickly, trying to think of a way out. The room was small, and more like a hospital room than a monster's den. Medical-grade lights stood in the corners. Beside the gurney was a silver tray, topped with several surgical instruments. The sight of their surfaces gleaming in the light sent her heart racing. She pulled at her straps, but couldn't break free. The leather held tough.

Behind her, somewhere beyond where she could turn her head, the creature was moving about, as if preparing some horrible ritual—maybe the same ritual it had used on Corey. It grumbled and then another voice broke in, this one female. "Everything alright?"

"Fine. I'm fine. This one's just a bit of a fighter, that's all. Help me get her into the machine, will you?"

There was a grating sound, like metal scraping against tile, and then it sounded like wheels were rolling across the floor. Tarrah's heart jumped into her throat when the monster brought another Velcro strap across her forehead. She screamed and tried to bite the monster again, but the female thing helping out held her head still, and the beast strapped her in tight. Tarrah couldn't move. She couldn't fight. All she could do was let her tears flow and pray that it would be over fast.

The female spoke again. "Did the cold help to slow them down? Damn things move so fast."

"Definitely. We'll use this method again. Just have to be careful not to slow their blood too much or we'll kill them off before we get what we need."

"Great. I'm going down the hall to give Fredrickson the news. Just shout if you need me."

The door clicked closed and the monster loomed over her, adjusting a strange, plastic dome-like device, so that it was around her head. "Please," she begged, hating that she had to beg something of such a horrible being. "Please let me go. I won't tell anyone about Corey, I promise. Just let me go."

A brief flicker of compassion crossed the beast's eyes. "I wish I could. But you don't understand. Your kind never does. We've been living in secrecy for so long. We need your blood. This is the only way. I'm sorry."

It moved out of her sight, but when it returned moments later, Tarrah's eyes locked on the instrument in its hand. Two large needles, attached to two long tubes. The monster was going to drain her, the way it had drained Corey. It was a miracle he'd survived as long as he had with that much blood loss. Tarrah screamed and strained against her restraints, but it was a useless fight. These beasts had this procedure down to a cruel science. She watched in horror as the monster brought the needles to her neck. She was going to die. There was no fixing it, no changing it. Her life was as good as over.

The monster whispered, "I hope you can understand. I wish I didn't have to hurt you. But it is necessary. I'm sorry. Take a deep breath. It'll all be over soon."

The tips of the needles pricked Tarrah's skin and she screamed.

Impossibly, she saw a familiar face appear behind the monster. It was pale and looked exhausted and sickly, but she'd never been so happy to see it, to see him. Even if she was wondering if he was only there to welcome her to the afterlife.

Then Corey opened his mouth, baring his fangs. He bit down hard on the monster's neck, and Tarrah watched in morbid fascination as the monster's skin paled and Corey's regained color. The monster breathlessly shouted something garbled, but Tarrah couldn't make out what it was supposed to be. It fell to the ground and Corey pushed the plastic dome away from her head and undid the straps that held her. She sat up and clung to him, reveling in the sensation of his heartbeat thumping gently against her chest once again. Her tears soaked his shirt, but after a moment, Corey pulled back and smiled into her eyes. His crystalline blue eyes were unmarred, so perfect with the lack of the black center the monster's eyes had. She couldn't ever remember being so happy to see them.

"You were dead. You looked dead, Corey. I thought—"

"It doesn't matter now. All that matters is that I'm not dead, and that we're together." He nodded toward the thing on the floor. It was gasping and struggling uselessly to crawl toward the door. The black circles in its eyes had grown huge. "I told you I had a plan. Luckily for us, feigning death worked. It didn't even bother to close the door when it carried you out."

She hugged him tightly, swearing never to let him go. He pulled back just a bit, brushing her hair from her eyes. "You should feed, Tarrah. And then we'll get out of here."

Slipping from the table, Tarrah crouched by the monster and opened her mouth to reveal her fangs. She couldn't remember ever being so hungry before. She looked into the beast's mouth as it gasped for air, at its strange, flat teeth. "It's weird, isn't it? I thought humans were just a myth. I mean, they were supposed to have died out so long ago. Who would've thought that they were real, and still around?"

Corey shrugged and licked his lips. "It is weird. Tasty though. Come on, babe. Drink up and let's go."

"Corey," she groaned, and looked up at her boyfriend of a hundred and fifty-three years. "Don't call me babe."

Then Tarrah bent over the terrified beast and bit into the warmth of his jugular vein.

A meal had never tasted so sweet.

Drama Queen's Last Dance

A Morganville Vampires Story

RACHEL CAINE

My name is Eve, and I am a drama queen.

I don't mean like any old garden-variety teen throwing a tantrum, oh no. I am a Drama Queen, with big initial capital letters and curlicues on top. I work hard at it, and I resent anybody lumping me in with a bunch of wannabe poseurs who haven't even qualified in Beginning Pouting, much less Champion Fit Throwing.

So when I had a golden opportunity for launching a big, fat, drama-filled scene, and ended up acting like an actual adult, perhaps you'll appreciate just how important this was to me. But wait, I'm getting ahead of myself.

First, let me explain the drama that is my life—and this is just the background, broad strokes, you know, for I am *epic*, I tell you. I am a Goth, but mainly for the fashion, not the 'tude. I had an emotionally abusive father and a checked-out mom. My little brother turned out to be one step short of either the asylum or federal prison.

Oh, and my boyfriend is a sweet boy, a gifted rock guitarist—and just happens to have an allergy to sunlight and crave plasma on a regular basis. However, in our home-town of Morganville this is not really all that unusual, since about a third of the citizens are vamps. Yes, vampires. Really. So you see why my life was generally a nightmare from an early age . . . the monsters under the bed really existed, and the pressure on all of us growing up was to give in. Be a good Morganville conformist.

Give up our blood for the cause.

Not me. I had a pact with all my other rebel friends. We'd never, ever be part of that scene.

And I mentioned my boyfriend is a vampire, right? Yeah. There's that.

Given all that, when I say that today was a *crisis* . . . well. Maybe you get the legendary scale of which I am speaking.

The saga started out a normal day—don't they all? I mean, surely one morning back there in prehistoric times a dinosaur woke up, yawned, chewed some coffee beans, and thought his day was going to be dead boring, just before a comet slammed into his neighborhood. "Normal day" in my life means that I wake up late, yell at my housemate Shane to get the hell out of my way as I dash to the bathroom in my vintage dragon-embroidered silk robe, and spend forty-five minutes doing shampoo, body wash, conditioner, blow dry, straightening, makeup, and clothes while I listen to Shane bang on the door and complain about how he is going to go pee all over my bedroom floor if I insist on living in the bathroom.

This morning I blew him a mocking black-lipsticked kiss on the way out, checked the time, and winced. I was late for my job at Common Grounds, the best local coffee shop of the two in town. (I also worked at the second best, but on alternate days.) I didn't mind dragging my ass in late to the University Center java store, but at Common Grounds, the boss was a little more of a leg-breaker—probably because he'd been making people show up on time since before the invention of the pocket watch.

I tried sneaking in the back door of Common Grounds, which seemed to work all right; I ditched my coffin purse in my locker, grabbed my long black apron, and tied it on before I went to grab a clipboard from the back. I took a hasty, not very thorough inventory, and toddled out to the front . . .

. . . Where my boss, Oliver, fixed me with a long, cold glare that had probably been terrifying underlings for hundreds of years. Oliver = vampire, obviously, although he did a good job of putting on a human smile and seeming like Mr. Nice Hippie Dude when he thought it would get him something. He wasn't bothering today, because the counter was slammed three deep with people desperate for their morning caff fix, and his other help, what's-her-name, Jodi-with-an-i, hadn't shown up yet. I held up my clipboard and put on my best innocent expression. "I was doing inventory," I said. "We need more lids."

He growled, and I could hear it even over the hissing brass monster of the espresso machine. "Get on the register," he snapped, and I could tell he wasn't buying the inventory excuse for a second. Well, it had been thin at best. I mouthed *sorry* and hurried over to beam a smile at the next harassed person who wanted to fork over four fifty for their mocha-chocalattefrappalicious, or whatever it was they'd ordered. We made things easy by charging one price for each size of drink, whatever it was. Funny how people never seemed to appreciate that time-saver. I worked fast, burning through the backlog of caffiends in record time, then moved to help Oliver build the drinks once the register was idle. He'd stopped growling, and from time to time actually gave me a nod of approval. This was, for Oliver, a little like arranging for a paid vacation and a dozen roses.

We'd gotten the morning rush out of the way and were settling into the slow midmorning period when a door in the back of the store opened, and a girl came strolling out. Now, that wasn't so unusual—that door was the typical vampire entrance, for those who wanted to avoid the not-so-healthful effects of a stroll in the sun. But I'd never seen this particular vamp before. She was . . . interesting. Masses of curly blonde hair that had that salon sheen you see in commercials but that hardly exists in the wild; porcelain-pale skin (without the benefit of the rice powder I was using); big jade-green eyes with spots of golden brown. She was wearing an Ed

Hardy tee under a black leather jacket, all buckles and zippers, and she looked pretty much like any other twenty-something in any town in the U.S., and maybe in a lot of the world. Shorter than most, maybe. She was five foot three, tops, but all kinds of curvy.

I took a cordial dislike to her, on principle, as she meandered her way toward the counter. Oliver, who'd been wiping down the bar, stopped in mid-motion to watch her. That seemed to be a male thing, because I noticed pretty much the entire Y chromosome population, including the table of gay boys, watching her, too. She didn't seem that sexy to me, at least in an obvious kind of way, and she wasn't vamping (no pun intended) it up . . . but she got attention, whether she was demanding it or not.

I wasn't used to being the wallflower, and it kinda pissed me off.

Still, I forced a smile as I went to the register. "Hi," I said, in my best professional welcome voice. "Can I help you?"

"I'll take this," Oliver said, and nudged me out of the way. He was smiling, which normally would be a bad sign, but this one went all the way to his eyes, and all of a sudden he didn't look like a vampire who would kick your ass, ra-a-a-ar, he looked like . . . a guy. Just a guy, kind of handsome in a sharp sort of way, although too old for me for sure.

The girl smiled back at him, and *wow*. I mean, it knocked me back a step, and I was (a) not male, and (b) not any kind of interested. "Oliver," she said, and even her voice was cute and small and sweet, with some kind of lilting accent that made her sound exotic and mysterious. Well, for Morganville, Texas, but then we find people from *Dallas* exotic and mysterious. "My dear friend, I haven't seen you in dark ages."

"Gloriana," he said. "I feared the worst, you know. It's cruel to keep us in suspense. Where were you?"

She shrugged and fiddled with the zippers on her jacket, looking coy as she shot him a look from beneath full, probably natural lashes. "After the last great war, I lost track of you, and the rest of our family," she said. "Those I found were—not healthy. I managed to avoid contracting the disease, but I didn't dare take the risk, so I stayed away."

"Where?"

"Oh, you know. Here and there. Europe. Australia was quite nice; I migrated here when they were still traveling by ocean liner. Since then, I've been drifting. I was recently in Los Angeles, where I ran into Bobby Sansome—you remember him?—and he told me almost everyone who was anyone was here, in Morganville. He also said that he'd come here to get the cure. I thought perhaps it was safe."

"It's safe," Oliver said. "But you'll need to present yourself to the Founder. There are rules of behavior in this town, accords you'll have to sign in order to stay. Understand?"

"Of course." Her charming smile got even wider. "Oliver, my sweet, do you really doubt that I know the rules of hospitality and good behavior? I haven't survived this long by preying indiscriminately on the livestock . . . oh." Her sparkling eyes flicked to me, inviting me to share the joke. "Not including you, naturally. I meant no offense."

"No?" I raised my eyebrows to let her know the sweet face didn't impress me. "That 'tude will get you in trouble around here."

Gloriana gave me an honestly puzzled look, then turned to Oliver. "What does she mean?"

"She means that humans have status here." He didn't look particularly happy about it, but then, that's Oliver for you. "You can't expect civility from them. And, unfortunately, you can't punish them for failing to provide it."

I snorted. "Bite me, fanger."

"See?"

Gloriana looked honestly taken aback for a few seconds and then smiled in what I could only call utter delight. Despite my best intentions, I got a traitorous little impulse to grin back. "Really? But this is *wonderful!*"

"It is?" It was Oliver's turn to look bemused, as if she'd suddenly started rattling on in a language he didn't recognize.

"Of course! You know I've never been terribly conventional, cuz. I'd be delighted to converse with humans again on an equal basis. Most of them are terribly dull, of course, but this one looks bright enough." Her green eyes swept over me, giving me the female X-ray of appraisal. "And certainly not afraid of controversy."

"*This one* is named Eve," I said. "And don't check my teeth like I'm your livestock. I bite back."

Gloriana laughed, an honest, full laugh, and I felt a shudder go through Oliver's body next to me. I couldn't tell what had brought *that* on—not fear, surely, the old dude didn't fear anybody that I could tell. "Eve," she said. "I'd like something to drink. Something hot and salty, perhaps in an O negative if you have it."

Ugh, but okay, I served vamps from time to time. I summoned up the professional smile again. "Sure thing. Coming right up."

It was only as I was warming up the blood out of the refrigerator that it occurred to me that she'd named my own blood type.

Hmmmm.

Coincidence. Probably.

Gloriana's visit to the coffee shop was eye-opening, to say the least. I put her blood in an opaque coffee cup, with a lid, and she and Oliver went to sit down together, presumably to jaw about old times, and I do mean *old* times. She wasn't stand-offish, the way some of the other vampires were—she said hello to people as they passed, gave them the same sweet smile, shook hands with a few.

I was pulling espresso shots for a mocha when my boy-friend came in the vampire entrance and got in the ordering line. I waved, and he winked at me. Michael is a total hottie, always has been; tall, blond, built, and shy, for the most part. He's always been more focused on music than the people around him, and from what he'd told me about how he'd come to get dead, that had been a real mistake. So he was trying to do a little better about connecting with people, as well as guitar riffs. He's always been my friend, but these days, he's a whole lot more than that.

I don't want to be sick about it, but I love him with my life. It scares me down to the bones to think about losing him—although in Morganville it's a lot more likely that *he'll* lose *me*, given the mortality rates among humans here.

Still.

I rushed through the next three orders to get to Michael and then took my time, leaning over the counter and smiling as our eyes met. "Hi, handsome," I purred. "See something you like?"

"Always," he said, and gave me just a flicker of that devastating Michael Glass grin. "And the coffee looks good, too."

"You are suave. I've always said so."

"And you're strange. But I love strange."

"Mmmm. Want to go take inventory with me in the back?"

"Isn't the boss here?" Michael made a show of looking around for Oliver.

He found him. He also spotted Gloriana, who was leaning her chin on her tiny little hand, looking at Oliver with luminous, big eyes.

"Wow," he said. This was not the thing you want to hear out of a boyfriend, believe me. "Who's the new girl?"

"Gloriana," I said. "She's not new. She's ancient." I was hoping that would put an end to it; Michael wasn't interested in hanging around other vampires, although he did it when circumstances required; he liked me, and Shane, and Claire. He liked us a whole lot better than the nonbreathers.

Until now, apparently. I could almost see the word balloon floating over his head: *should go say hello*. But he was smart enough not to say it. With an effort, he dragged his attention away from Gloriana and looked at me again. "So, you have plans for lunch today?"

"Nope. I was thinking about a smoothie." In this coffee bar, you had to be sure you were grabbing the pureed strawberries, and not, you know, something else, but the smoothies were pretty awesome. "I could be talked into something non-food-related, though."

"Shane's at work," Michael said. "Claire's at school. House is empty. I could make you something hot."

He said it straight-faced; that was the wonderful, wicked thing about Michael, he could deliver the most outrageous lines with utmost sincerity. It left me wondering if I was the only one with my mind in the gutter . . . until I spotted the amusement in his clear blue eyes.

"I'll bet," I breathed. "Meet you there at one o'clock, okay?"

"Not twelve?"

"I came in late."

"Ah. I'll keep myself occupied."

"Hey!"

He gave me the full, devastating smile and leaned across the counter to kiss me. His lips were cool and sweet and softer than they had any right to be, but he was gone before I could really savor it.

He'd left four fifty on the counter—his way of saying that I should have a drink myself. Which I did, making it extra sweet and extra strong, like him.

It was only as I was sipping the drink that I realized Gloriana was staring at the door through which Michael had gone. She finally leaned over and pecked Oliver on both cheeks in a European sort of farewell and took her cup of O to go . . . following Michael.

I didn't like that.

At all.

One o'clock crawled slowly toward me, to the point where I checked the coffee shop's clock against my cell phone *and* my watch, just to be sure. When the hand finally dragged itself to twelve forty-five, I stripped off my apron and chirped to Oliver, "Lunch!"

"Don't you have time to make up?" he asked, not looking away from the cash he was counting for the bank bag.

"Yeah, I'll stay late."

"I'd rather you worked through lunch."

"Sorry, slavery's gone out of fashion," I said, and hung up my apron on the old coat tree at the end of the counter. "Gotta run."

He grunted and waved his hand. I retrieved my purse from the locker and dashed out.

It wasn't a long walk home, but it was unexpectedly chilly; rain clouds were rolling in, dark and ominous, and the wind had kicked up. It blew sand and broken bits of grass across the roads, rippled the leaves on the trees, and generally made walking less fun than usual. I was happy to turn down Lot Street and see my big, shiny black hearse parked at the curb. Death's party bus. Holla.

I couldn't wait and broke into a jog up the walk, the steps, and across the porch, and unlocked the front door as fast as I could. *Yes!* I slammed the door and threw my stuff on the hall table; Michael's keys were already there, in the candy dish. My heartbeat sped up even faster. "Let's get the party started!" I called, and walked down the narrow hallway toward the living room.

On the way there, I passed the formal parlor room, which was basically a furniture museum; we never sat in there. Except this time I registered people in there as I passed. I stopped, backed up, and found Michael sitting in the big red velvet wing chair.

Gloriana was sitting on the settee, her to-go cup on the marble coffee table. She had her legs crossed, and seemed *very* comfortable.

In my house.

With my boyfriend.

"Michael?" I asked. He stood up, looking guilty and nervous, which was new for him. "What's going on?"

"Uh . . . this is Gloriana."

"I know who she is. I told *you* who she was."

"Eve," Gloriana said, all warmth and sweetness and apology. "I only wanted to meet Michael, as he's Amelie's newest child. I am a curious creature, I know. I mean nothing by it."

"Eve, chill," Michael said. "She just came over to say hello."

"I see." My voice sounded flat and pissed, even to my own ears. "That's great. Now she can just say good-bye, too."

"I meant no offense, most surely. Here, I'll be going." Gloriana stood up and extended her hand to Michael, knuckles turned up. "It was charming to meet you, Michael Glass."

He took her hand and looked briefly confused about what to do, then lifted it very formally to his lips and kissed her knuckles. Not *kissed* kissed, more of a brush of his lips, but it still made me feel lightheaded and sick inside. "Welcome to Morganville," he said. "Hope to see you around."

"Oh, I'm sure you will," Gloriana laughed. "After all, the sign says *you'll never want to leave*, isn't that true? I already find much to like about Morganville." She flicked those green eyes toward me. "Eve. Thank you for your hospitality."

"Yeah. Don't forget to take your blood with you."

Michael gave me a look. I gave him one right back. While we were doing the silent stare thing, Gloriana retrieved her cup and headed for the door. Michael moved past me to open it for her and handed her a big, floppy black coat and hat to throw on. "There's an entrance to the underground a block down," he said. "Look for the glyph. You can bring the coat and hat back later."

"Thank you," she said, and swaddled herself up in the sun-defying garb. She looked like a waif playing dress-up. "You are so kind, Michael." She pronounced it French, like *Meeshell*. "I will return the kindness soon."

He watched her go. I watched him watch her go, and then he shut the door, locked it, and without looking at me said, "So, just how mad are you?"

Without a word, I turned and walked down the hall, into the kitchen, and poured myself a glass of water. I wasn't thirsty, but there was a burning pain in my throat, and besides, it gave me something to do with my shaking hands.

I heard the door open as Michael followed me in. "Seriously," he said. "Eve, I was just being friendly. She's new in town."

"Oh, so the hand-kissing, that's just being friendly? I never see you doing it to Oliver."

"A lot of these older vamp women, it's what they expect. They don't shake hands, Eve."

"Well, they need to bring their undead asses into the twenty-first century, then, because hand-kissing went out with the guillotine, didn't it? And since when do you do what's *expected*, anyway?"

Michael shook his head and leaned back against the counter. "It's not like that."

"Like *what*?"

"Like I want to take her to bed, which is what you're thinking, Eve."

I couldn't believe he'd gone and said that right out loud, even if I *was* thinking it. Not in such polite terms, though. "Then what's it like?"

"Like I'm—curious. Look, she's friendly, not like a lot of the others. I can ask her things, about being—" There was more color in his cheeks than normal; that was the closest a vampire can come to blushing. "About being what I am."

"What kind of things?" I demanded.

Michael met my eyes. "Like how likely I am to lose control and hurt somebody close to me. That kind of thing. Especially when I'm hungry and we're together."

Oh. That hurt, in all kinds of unexpected ways; these were personal things, and it wasn't just personal for him. *I* was the one who'd drawn the line with him, who'd said I was never, ever going to let him bite me, especially not that way. And it wasn't something we talked about, not ever. Especially not with third parties who might be named Sexy Hell Kitten. "And you thought it was okay to discuss all this with a vamp you met, like, thirty seconds ago."

"We've been talking for an hour, Eve. It wasn't the first thing out of my mouth."

I swallowed. "Did you kiss her?"

"Eve!"

"Did you?"

"Jesus, of course not."

"Did you want to?"

Michael just looked at me for a few fatal seconds, then said, "She's got that effect on guys, so yeah, I guess I thought about it. But I didn't do it."

That didn't make me feel any better. Gloriana would be back. At the very least, she'd return the hat and coat, and if I wasn't here, he'd get all cozy with her again, and . . . things could happen. It wasn't that I didn't trust Michael, I did, I really did, but . . . she wasn't just any random chick. She hadn't stopped in just to pay a social call; Gloriana was hunting.

She was stalking my boyfriend.

"Over my dead body," I murmured. Michael looked startled. "Sorry. Talking to myself."

He sighed, straightened up, and crossed to stand right in front of me. He took the water glass out of my hand and put it carefully on the counter, then leaned in and kissed me, sweet and hot and hard. He braced himself with his hands on either side of me on the counter, and *damn*, the white fire of that just about wiped out anything else I had on my mind, including Gloriana's sly, sweet smile, or the way Michael had looked after her when she'd gone.

He was mine. *Mine.*

His hands left the counter and stroked through my hair, down the column of my neck, spread out on my shoulders. My top was stretchy enough to slide down my arms under the pressure of his palms, and I shivered as cool air hit my skin.

Michael picked me up in his arms like I was a bag of air, and for a long second he looked down at my face. His expression left me breathless. "You know I love you," he said. "You know that, don't you?"

"I know," I said. "But I also know that can change."

"Never," he said, and kissed me again. "Never."

And for a little while, as he carried me upstairs to his room, I believed that would actually be true.

Always.

Even when I felt the tangle of frustration in him when his teeth grazed my neck and he didn't bite.

I didn't hear about Gloriana for three days, until Michael told me there was going to be a big to-do in Founder's Square on Friday night to welcome the newest arrival. He had an invitation, of course; all the vampires got them. Some humans did, too, including our bookworm housemate Claire . . . who, not surprisingly, decided that our *other* housemate Shane would be her plus one to the party. I was kind of shocked that Claire decided to go, though; she wasn't generally the dressed-up party type (or the dressed-down party type, come to that).

"Oh, I met her," Claire said, as we were doing laundry in the basement of the Glass House. She was sitting on the dryer this time while I dumped dirties into the washer; as usual, she was reading, this time one of Charlaine Harris's vampire books. She probably considered it research. "Gloriana, I mean. She seems nice."

Nice? I almost dropped the laundry detergent on my toes, which wouldn't have been as much of an owie as you might think, since my boots are steel-toed. "How'd you run into her?"

"She visited Myrnin."

That was strange, because Amelie was really damn serious that nobody, but nobody, visited Myrnin; those of us who knew Claire's boss at all had sworn under pain of actual, bloody death not to talk about him, ever, to anybody not in the know. Gloriana just strolling in to the equivalent of a highly secure facility seemed . . . unlikely.

Except that I'd met her, too. Gloriana seemed like she could charm her way into Fort Knox, and the guards would stand in line to help her carry out the gold. "How'd they get along?" I asked.

"Oh, he was all suave," Claire said, and all but giggled. "He actually ran off and got dressed up for her. It was cute. Well, I can understand why, she's pretty . . . pretty. They know each other, from olden times. Maybe he dated her once."

"Maybe," I said. Weirder things had happened. "So, you liked her?"

Claire turned her head and looked at me; she'd gotten her shoulder-length hair cut again, shorter, but it was messy from the wind outside. Still cute, though. Her big, brown eyes were way too smart for either of our good. "You didn't?"

I hadn't told her about Gloriana's visit to the house. I wasn't sure why; I usually come right out with my latest drama, but this had felt . . . more dire than usual. And really personal. Now, I just shook my head and focused on adding detergent in the right amounts for the colored clothes. Although I was tempted to bleach the hell out of Michael's stuff. "You ever have that happen where you meet someone and just—clash? We were like a gravel and cream sandwich."

"That is the weirdest thing you've ever said. I suppose you were the cream?"

"Of course I was the cream. Sha."

Trust Claire to not get distracted. "Something happened with her and Michael," she said. Wow. Zero to correct in one point nothing seconds. "Right?"

"Do you really think I'm that shallow that—okay, yes. She came over here. I found the two of them together."

Her eyes widened, and she slipped down off the dryer. "Seriously, *together*? Like—"

"No, not like. Tea in the parlor, or the vampy equivalent. You know. Sitting, talking." I frowned. "But it was way too nice. And besides, here, he's *mine*. You know?"

Claire nodded, not that it made the least bit of sense. She's a good friend. "Did you talk to him about it?"

"Oh, sure. Nothing happened, yadda yadda. The usual. But my maydar went off like crazy."

"Maydar?"

"As in, he *may* be thinking about super hot sex with her. Like radar, only not as sure."

Claire rolled her eyes. "Did you *ask*?"

"Yes," I said. "I asked."

"And?"

"And he took me to bed."

"Oh."

"Yeah." I frowned unhappily down at clothes, slammed the lid, and turned on the washer. "Oh. Exactly."

"Exactly what?"

That was Michael, standing at the top of the basement steps. Claire and I did the guilty dance. She dropped her book, and hurriedly picked it up. "Nothing," I blurted. My cheeks felt warm, and I was glad I was in shadow until I remembered, duh, vampire eyes. "Girl talk."

He nodded, looking at me with a little sadness in his gaze, I thought. "Just wanted to remind you that we're out of milk again. And hot sauce."

"Why are those two always out at the same time? Because those do *not* go together."

"I suspect Shane. He'd put hot sauce in anything," Michael said.

"Ugh," Claire sighed. "So true." Michael didn't leave, and after a second, Claire cleared her throat, closed up her book, and said, "Yeah, I've got something to do. Upstairs. Away from here."

He stepped aside to let her out, then closed the door behind her and settled down on the steps. I had wet whites to put in the dryer, so I busied myself with that, making extra sure that everything was untangled, that the dryer sheet was in, that the timer was just so.

Michael waited patiently for me to get the fidgeting done before he said, "If you don't want to go to the party, just say so."

"Of course I want to go. It's a big swanky dress-up party. How often do I get to go to those, in Morganville? And I mean, some of these vampires own their own tuxes, even."

"Eve." His voice was gentle, and very kind. "I mean it. If you don't want to go, we won't go."

"I can't avoid her forever. It's too small a town."

He couldn't argue with that, and didn't try. "That doesn't mean you have to go to her welcome party. And if you want, I'll dress up and take you out somewhere nice."

"Nice being a relative term around here," I said, but secretly, the idea that he was willing to put on a suit and take me to the all-night diner made me smile. "Thanks, sweetie. But maybe I should just suck it up and go. What could happen?"

"Oh, plenty," he said cheerfully enough. And he was right. The two of us had rarely been to a party that *hadn't* ended in some kind of disaster, whether it was the senior prom where Chuck (aptly named) Joris had vomited in the punchbowl, or the EEK fraternity party, which had ended in a vampire attack. And let's not even *mention* Mr. Evil Vampire Bishop's big welcome party, which had been a truckload of trouble.

"I'll be fine," I said, and glared at the clothes tumbling on high heat. "I'll play nice as long as she does."

I turned around. Michael had come down the stairs and crossed the distance between us, noiseless as the air, and I melted into his arms with a sense of real relief.

He kissed the top of my head. "That's my lady."

I really hoped he meant that.

C⁓

I woke up the next day expecting—oh, I don't know, doom, disaster, and Apocalypse; weirder things had happened in this town. But things seemed normal enough, even after I left the house and headed off to the day job. The one not-so-great thing that happened was that when I got to Common Grounds, guess who was there?

Gloriana. Deep in conversation with about a half dozen admirers. She'd picked one of the tables in the darker section of the room, far away from the blazing sunlight, and at first I thought all her new groupies were vamps, but no, some of them were definitely still rocking a pulse. A couple of them were college boys, complete with the ubiquitous backpacks. I was pretty sure one of them was Monica Morrell's future ex-boyfriend, what's-his-name, the football player. Oooh, the fur would fly if Monica dropped in and saw her current squeeze crushing on the New Girl.

I was kind of hoping for that, but no such luck. Gloriana hung out for hours, laughing and talking, ordering regular rounds of whatever.

When she finally left, I saw Oliver watching her with a troubled look on his face. "Boss?" I asked. "Something wrong?"

"No," he said. "No, I don't think so. Not yet, at any rate."

No matter how much extra effort I put into customer service, he wouldn't elaborate, and that bothered me because (a) Oliver was pretty free with his criticisms for the most part, and (b) it wasn't like him to look worried. Ever.

No Apocalypse had been declared by the end of my shift, though.

I supposed that qualified as a win.

Gloriana's party that night was fabulous, from the raised-ink invitations on paper so soft and thick it felt like skin (but wasn't, thankfully), to the uniformed vampire doormen on duty at the party building, to the china and crystal and candles on the round banquet tables inside. The vampires had turned out in force; I guess they didn't get much chance to party like it was 1499 either. I was wearing a slinky black velvet dress, with a train that trailed behind me like a fan. It was cut low in the back to show off the rose tattoo I had there, and although I didn't have any really good jewelry, I'd bummed some pretty good costume stuff off of people I knew. I looked fab.

Although in the company of vampires, I looked like . . . lunch. But if there was one thing I knew about Morganville, it was that your risk of being lunch was pretty much the same whether you were dressed like a movie star or a bag lady. Better to go out in style, if you had to go.

For all that, if Michael hadn't been on my arm, the look I got coming into the ballroom might have made me turn around and run.

Luckily, Michael stayed steady and whispered, "Easy. They're not going to hurt us." It was the *us* that did it— the fact that we were a unit, and he didn't even try to think about it any other way. I took a deep breath, put on a brave smile, and raised my chin. That put my veins on display, but whatever.

Michael was wearing a nice black suit and a tie that wasn't quite conventional, in this crowd, but he didn't give a damn. Anyway, it was a music tie. They could munch ass if they didn't approve.

There was a line of vampires to meet, some I already knew and some I didn't. I took my cue from Michael about how respectful to be, but not because I felt particularly humble; many of these old-school vamps took offense easily. When I got to Amelie and Oliver, I breathed a sigh of relief.

They might take offense, but I knew what I could get away with.

I shook Amelie's hand firmly. She was wearing white gloves, and I was pretty sure the diamonds around her wrists were real. The gown was ice blue, and really beautiful, and probably by some famous designer I'd never heard about. Oliver was in a tuxedo, with tails. Damn, he James Bonded up really well. He bent over my hand, just a little—more of a suggestion of a hand kiss than anything else.

And then there was Gloriana, in a deep, vivid red gown, laughing and flirting with a whole circle of male admirers, both vamp and human. I saw Richard Morrell, the mayor, right in there, while his sister Monica stood off to the side, looking deeply unhappy. She was used to being the belle of the ball, and she'd certainly dressed for it, but whatever she was wearing, it looked like a knockoff rag next to Gloriana's dress, and she knew it. She also was alone, which was very unusual indeed. Even at a vampire party, she would have expected to draw some male attention, but there was a brand-new queen bee in town.

I felt Michael slowing as we passed Gloriana's group, as if he was reluctant to miss the opportunity, but he kept going. We went to the punch table, which featured two kinds— with plasma, and without. He poured mine first. When I looked over at him, his face looked paler than normal, and the pupils of his eyes had gone wide, even in the relatively bright light.

"What?" I asked him.

"Nothing."

Shane squired Claire over to join us, already scanning the edible snacks with the eye of a kid who'd grown up snatching food where he could. He grabbed a plate and filled it until Claire slapped his hand. "You're not starving," she said. "Come on."

"It's been a long time since lunch," Shane said. "So yeah, I am, Slappy Girl. Do you want one of these or not?" He held up a carrot stick. When she nodded, he fed it to her. Awww. So cute. "All right, you are now a party to the overindulgence. Quiet."

Claire, bless her, had somehow blackmailed Shane into donning a suit jacket, at least, although the pants looked suspiciously like dark jeans. At least he'd left the tuxedo T-shirt at home. The vamps wouldn't have been amused. He was even wearing a tie, though it featured Bettie Page in a lot of provocative poses. I hoped Oliver hadn't noticed.

"Did you see Gloriana?" Claire asked her boyfriend. Shane—big, scruffy Shane, who was cute in a totally different way than Michael, but really, just about as sweet—looked down at her and cocked one eyebrow.

"Am I alive?" he asked, and put his hand over his heart. "Yep, I noticed her. Oh, sorry, Mikey. No offense to the unalive."

Michael would normally have flipped him off—best-friends love—but he just gave Shane a look. Not his normal look, either. "Watch yourself with her," Michael said. "There's something . . . not right about her."

"Dude, she *looks* very right." Shane lost his humor and started to frown. "Are you okay?"

"I can feel—" Michael shut his eyes tightly. "I can feel her from here. It's like a . . . call. A pull."

His hand was tight on mine, so tight it was painful, and I gave a little squeak of pain. When his eyes opened, they were crimson, and his pupils had shrunk down to small pinpoints.

I turned and looked. Gloriana was standing up. The men crowding around her were backing off, making . . . an exit. She smiled at them and glided out, hardly seeming to touch the floor as she went.

She headed straight for us.

For Michael.

She was wearing red gloves, and her diamonds, just like Amelie's, were real. Her smile was brighter than the glitter of the jewels. "Michael," she said, and took his hands in hers. He dropped mine so fast it was as if he'd forgotten I was there, and leaned in. She air-kissed him on both cheeks. He didn't pull back very far, and she didn't let go of his hands. "So glad you came to my party. It wouldn't have been a welcome without you, *mon chere*." She did let go then, but only to reach up and touch his eyelids to close them. "You're going too far. Control. You must learn control."

He was shuddering very slightly, but when she stepped back, he opened his eyes, and the red was almost gone. Almost. "Thanks," he said. His voice sounded rough in his throat. "Have you met my friends? You remember Eve . . ."

Somehow, having my name follow the word "friends" didn't make me feel any better at all. I didn't say anything. Neither did Gloriana, who just nodded very slightly. I couldn't tell what she felt about me, if she felt anything at all.

"And this is Claire—"

"Yes, we've met," Gloriana said. Her voice was warm and very sweet. "How is dear Myrnin? I thought he would be here tonight."

"He doesn't do parties, mostly," Claire said. She seemed kind of charmed by Gloriana's make-nice attitude, which was surprising; Claire was usually more level-headed than that. "Well, neither do I, really. Oh, this is Shane, by the way. My boyfriend."

"Charming," Gloriana said, and extended her hand to him, knuckles up. Shane, who looked just about as overcome as every other guy in the room, took it and shook vigorously. Gloriana looked, just for a moment, taken aback, and then she smiled, again. "Very direct, I see."

"I'm not subtle," Shane agreed. "You're very pretty."

Claire dug her elbow into his side. He didn't seem to notice. Gloriana's smile grew wider. "Yes," she said. "I'm afraid I am. It's a bit of a curse, sometimes." She turned back to Michael, who was still treating me like a nonperson, and held out her fingers. "Perhaps you'll save me from this sea of admirers," she said. "And escort me to the dance floor."

I opened my mouth, then closed it, because without a glance at me, Michael walked her past me, out to the open area of the ballroom, and the musicians struck up some kind of a waltz. And that wasn't Michael. It just . . . wasn't.

She was doing this to him.

As I looked around, I saw it on the faces of the guys who'd been hovering around her earlier—a kind of lost longing, as if she was the only girl in the world. I even saw it on the faces of guys I would have sworn knew better, like Richard Morrell.

It was creepy, to the power of actively sinister.

Claire put her arm around me. "Hey," she said softly. "Are you okay?"

I was, surprisingly. "That bitch is going down," I said. "She is *not* taking my boyfriend for a party favor."

"Chill, she's just dancing with him," Shane said. He was watching Gloriana with that same eerie, distracted concentration, and now Claire noticed it, too, with appropriate levels of alarm.

"No, she's not," Claire said, and smacked his arm. "Hey!"

"Oh, sorry," Shane said, and then looked around. "Right. Michael, not a party favor . . . How exactly are we going to accomplish that? Because she's wearing him like a paper hat right now."

I marched right over to the receiving line, grabbed Oliver's hand, and said, "Dance with me."

He gave me a long, odd look, exchanged a glance with Amelie, who seemed amused, and finally said, "If you insist."

"I do," I said. "Come on."

In my heels, I was almost a match for Oliver in height. The last thing I wanted to be doing was clutching his undead body and twirling around on the dance floor, but I needed to keep Gloriana in sight, and I needed information. Oliver was a two-in-one.

And surprisingly, my vampire boss could *dance*. Like, reality-show-winning dancing. He whirled me around like an expert, and all I needed to do was pay attention and relax. That was a lot more fun than it should have been.

"Now," he said, about a minute or so into the ballroom display, "what exactly do you want from me?"

"Gloriana," I said, a little breathlessly. "I need to know what her deal is. Now."

Oliver glanced over at Gloriana, who was clinging to my boyfriend like red moss on a tree. Michael looked dazed. She looked delighted. "Ah," he said. "Gloriana doesn't like to be alone. I think she's decided that Michael is her newest accessory."

"He didn't want to go," I said. "She did something to him. I saw it. Some kind of . . . vampire superpower."

"Glamour," he said. "Most vampires have it, to some extent, though we rarely bother to use it. Gloriana is one of the few that has it in strength, and can use it on her own kind."

"Not cool."

"Not illegal," he corrected. "She'll tire of him soon enough, in a year or two. My advice is to let her have him, rather than risk becoming her enemy. He'll come back to you. Perhaps a bit worse for wear, but—"

"No," I said. My cheeks felt like they were flaming under the pale makeup. "No way in hell. He is *my* boyfriend, and she doesn't get to play with him. It'd be different if he wanted it, but he doesn't."

Oliver gave me a dark, pitying smile and bent me over backward. "Are you absolutely sure of that?" he asked. "Because Gloriana can only work that kind of glamour on those who are open to it. Michael's a new vampire. He's never been with one of us. I'm sure he has . . . questions."

He did. He'd told me that, straight up, and now it scared me. "I'm sure," I said. My eyes filled with tears. "But he can't just . . . take off with her. He loves me."

Oliver let me up—or rather, snapped me back upright—and glided me backwards through a complicated set of twirls. "I'm afraid that love is rarely that simple," he said. "Or that painless. Ah, look, they're leaving."

I caught my breath on a cry and pulled free of him, or tried to; he held on long enough to say, "Don't get into the middle of it, Eve. The pull's strong. Michael may not be able to resist no matter what you do." He smiled, a little sadly. "You may take that from one who knows."

I yanked my wrist free, gathered up my train, and dashed out of the door after Gloriana and Michael.

This was the moment when I had a choice to make. I knew what I *wanted* to do . . . scream, cry, start a slap-fight with the undead skank trying to take my boyfriend. But somehow, I knew that fighting for Michael that way would only make me look small, petty, and ugly beside Gloriana's mature poise.

I didn't know what the alternative was, but I was going to have to find it, fast.

They were halfway down the steps when I caught up. The light out here was mostly provided by the white ghostly moon, and they looked identically pale as they turned to look at me as I rushed down toward them. "Michael!" I gasped, coming to a halt one step above them. "Michael, please wait!"

Gloriana smiled at me, still maddeningly sweet. I'd been talking to him, but she was the one who answered me. "Oh, don't worry, I'll bring him back," she said. "If he wants to return."

"Go back, Eve," Michael said. "I'll see you later."

"You mean, you'll dump me later?" I felt short of breath. Suffocating. "No. If you want to break up, be a man. Do it now, to my face."

"I don't want to hurt you," he said, and I believed that. I could see it on his face. "I can't do this right now, all right? Just go home. I'm not—"

"Not yourself? Yeah, that's because *she's* leading you around by the—by the nose! Please, *listen*! I love you. I know you don't want to do this to me. Or to yourself."

Gloriana wasn't smiling anymore. I could feel the waves of pressure coming off of her, closing around Michael. She was working hard at this, I realized. Harder than she'd expected. I might have taken some satisfaction in that, except I was terrified that all her effort might actually be enough. "Michael," she said. "Tell her to go away and go back to her *friends*. She's just a child. You need someone . . . more experienced. Someone who understands what you want, what you need, and isn't afraid to help you through this . . . difficult time."

He didn't say anything. That, in itself, was a victory, but I could see him shaking again, very lightly. Vibrating, really. When she laid her gloved fingers on his hand, I saw his lips part in a soundless gasp.

"No," I said, and took a step down, putting myself on the same level with him. I knocked her hand away, wrapped my arms around him. "No, I'm not going anywhere. You've got a room full of candidates back there. You don't get him, not unless you go through me first."

Gloriana backed off, frowning. God, even her frowns were adorable, though the anger brewing in her eyes wasn't so precious. I'd surprised her, all right. And now she was starting to realize that she might not be able to hijack Michael the way she'd planned . . . and she wasn't pleased. Not at all.

Michael stopped shaking, and I felt him relax against me. Sweet relief. His head came down on my shoulder, and I turned my head to glare at the other vampire. She was expressionless now, not smiling, not laughing, not exuding charm. She looked like a wax doll, and not a particularly pretty one, at that.

"Is that how it's going to be?" she asked.

Michael pulled in a breath and said, "I'm with Eve." Just that. Just three words, but they made me feel faint with relief and love.

I didn't let go of him.

Gloriana slowly, reluctantly, smiled, and the prettiness came back. "I apologize," she said. "My mistake, of course. I didn't think you were serious about her, or that she'd be so . . . forceful. I misjudged you both." She put her palms together and bowed—mockingly, I was almost sure. "I'm sure we'll see each other again, Michael. Eve."

He didn't answer her. He was frighteningly quiet, I thought. Gloriana looked up, toward the top of the steps, and I saw her face momentarily change into something that was very, very ugly.

Amelie was standing up there, shining in the moonlight, radiantly silver. Beautiful in a way that Gloriana would never be, for all her charm and good looks.

"Come back to the party," Amelie said. "Your swains are missing you, Glory. I'm sure you wouldn't want to be responsible for any more broken hearts tonight."

She turned and walked away, and I heard Gloriana make a light hissing sound, almost like a snake. She gave Michael one last, sidelong look, and then I felt something . . . snap, as if pressure had broken around us.

As she walked away, Michael tightened his arms around me, almost lifting me off my feet, and whispered, "God, Eve . . . God, I'm so sorry." He was shaken, and he sounded angry—not at me, but at himself. "I couldn't stop myself. It was like being . . . It was like a dream. But I didn't want to wake up, either."

"Oliver called it glamour," I said. "I can't feel it, though."

"No, not unless she wants you to. She's . . . narcotic. It's terrible, but it . . . feels so good."

I closed my eyes for a moment and strangled my inner drama queen before I said, very carefully, "Michael, if you really . . . need her . . ."

Michael Glass raised his head. The moonlight was shining full on his face, and I could read everything there, all the conflict and the love and the desperation. "I want you," he said. "I want to stay with you. I love you. God, Eve, I love you."

The intensity of the way he said it made my heart lurch painfully. I wanted to cry in relief, but I managed to hold the tears back. "Then don't do that again," I said. "Promise."

"No," he said. "You promise *me* something."

I blinked. "I . . . promise never to dance with Oliver again?"

He didn't laugh. "Promise me you'll marry me," he said. "Promise me that you're not going to leave me. I need you, Eve, I've always needed you and I always will. Please. Promise me."

I wasn't sure I'd heard him right, not at first. *Marry*. It wasn't that I hadn't thought about it, dreamed about it, but . . . hearing him say it, right out loud, that was . . . terrifying. And thrilling. And terrifying, again.

I didn't know what to say, except, finally, "Yes." It came out a whisper, timid and slow, but it seemed to ring like a bell on the still air. I said it again, stronger. "Yes. Oh, God, *yes*."

He kissed me. It wasn't his normal kind of sweet, gentle kiss—this was full of the same intensity, the same desperate focus. All of a sudden, I wanted him in all kinds of ways, with identical ferocity. He was growling a little, in the back of his throat, and sliding his hands down my arms.

Then he picked me up and carried me down the steps, into the shadows. It was wild, and crazy, and stupid, but neither of us cared just then; we just *needed*.

And as always, that critical moment came, when his teeth grazed my neck. I thought about Gloriana, about that need inside him she'd used against him. I thought about all my long-held vows to myself, and weighed all that against how much I loved him.

I put my hand on his cheek. "Michael." He licked my skin, just above the veins. "Michael, do it. Go ahead."

For a second he didn't move, and then he slowly pulled away and looked down at me. I couldn't read his expression. "You're sure," he said. "You're really sure."

"I'm sure. Just, you know, don't—" *Kill me,* I thought. My heartbeat was thumping so fast it sounded like war drums. "I don't want to be turned. You know that."

"I know," he said, very softly. "One more time. You're sure."

"Yes." This time, I heard certainty in my own voice, and a kind of peace settled over me. "Yes."

I can't remember what it felt like, not really; it was overwhelming, and scary, and wonderful, and so, so much better than I'd ever imagined. He licked the wound gently, until the bleeding stopped, and then gently kissed it. I felt dizzy and woozy and unbelievably high—vampire bites can do that, if they do it right. If they take the time. Or so I'd heard.

I sank against Michael's chest, and he held me. "Okay?" he whispered. I made a wordless sound of pleasure and snuggled in against him. He smiled. "Thank you."

I laughed. "It wasn't a gift, Michael."

He kissed my nose. "No," he agreed. "But you are. I don't know what I'd be without you, Eve. But I don't want to find out."

"Not even if Gloriana comes calling?"

"Especially if Gloriana comes calling," he said, very seriously. "You were amazing, by the way. You made her look . . ."

"Cheap?" I said cheerfully.

"Immature," he said, and kissed my hand. "You looked like the sexiest woman in the world."

"Well, in fairness, I *am* the sexiest woman in the world."

"And you're always right."

"You are so brilliant to recognize that."

He helped me to my feet and got handsy settling my dress back around me comfortably. Then he held me in place and stared down at me for a long moment.

"Am I really sexier than Gloriana?" I asked.

And that got me a slow, *very* sexy smile. "Sorry, don't think I know anyone by that name."

And then he took off his suit jacket, wrapped it around my shoulders, and walked me back up to the party.

Thief

JERI SMITH-READY

Everything's better on the road.

Take rainbows. The ones up in the sky just sorta sit there. But the ones on the highway—spiking up through the water tossed by the tires? They dance and shimmer and hurry along with us. They're going places.

I leaned my elbows on the barrier between the school bus stairs and the front seat, staring at the rainbow following the silver minivan ahead of us.

One, two, three, four, five, six . . .

The bus peeled off at the exit. I kept counting, watching the rainbow, twisting a lock of my hair, sticky with curling gel. *Seven, eight, nine, ten, eleven.*

I craned my neck, but the rainbow disappeared from sight. I sank back into my seat, my stomach heavy. An even number of seconds meant good luck, but an odd number? Well, it would've been better if I'd never seen the rainbow at all.

As the bus turned onto our road, something hit the back of my head, too big to be a spitball. I pulled the crumpled paper from my thick blonde curls, which had gone frizzy in the South Carolina humidity. I figured it was another nasty note calling me Traveller trash or Gypsy whore. Country folk kids weren't real creative.

It wasn't a note. It was a ten-dollar bill. Okay, maybe they were getting more creative.

The bus clanged with my classmates' cackles. I glanced at the driver, who kept her eyes on the road. Yep. Everyone—teachers, principals, cops—looks the other way when country folk harass Travellers. They figure we got it coming.

I turned to scan the crowd of smug faces. That stupid sophomore Eric Scheier was grinning at me from four rows back. I wanted to give him the finger, but I knew that would be the moment the bus driver would miraculously regain her sight.

So I gave Eric my coldest, meanest, most brain-splitting vampire glare. Which would've knocked him on his butt, had I actually been a vampire.

Eric put up his hands all fake innocent, and laughed some more.

The bus jerked to a stop at my corner. It was "my" corner because I was the only one in our Traveller group who went to the public high school. Heck, I was one of maybe half a dozen out of hundreds who went to any high school.

I scooped up my bag, then stalked back to Eric. I leaned over and smoothed the ten-dollar bill across his chest. "You dropped this, honey."

He ripped his gaze up from my boobs to my face. Beside him, his girlfriend, Sally, scowled at his horndog eyes.

"Cassie, you oughta thank me," he said. "I'm saving you the trouble of stealing it."

I leaned over further, whispering in his ear. "How many times I gotta tell you?" I slid the bill up and tucked it into the top of his polo shirt. "We ain't. All. Thieves."

"Miss O'Riley, you get off this bus!" the driver called. "I got a schedule to keep."

"Sure thing." I picked up my bag, dropping Eric's wallet inside, and strode off the bus, back into my world.

It's true what I said, that not all Irish Travellers are thieves. Thanks to the media and a few big arrests by the feds (I miss you, Granddad!), people think all any of us do is run scams and pick pockets.

But it's not totally true. Travellers just have a bad reputation. One we O'Rileys aim to live up to.

The sun was shining even hotter now, like it was trying to one-up the rain. I sighed with relief to get under the shade of the oak trees, even though the Spanish moss was dripping like crazy on the sidewalk.

Behind me I heard one of my favorite sounds in the world—the engine of an Audi S-4. I pulled back my shoulders and added extra swing to my hips.

"Hey there, darlin'," drawled the honey-soaked voice. "You need a date tonight?"

I lifted my chin and went full-on Southern Belle. "Ah'm sorry, sir, but I'm spoken for on this fine evening."

"How spoken for?"

"A fair young gentleman has secured my hand in marriage."

"Does this boy know how lucky he is?"

"I don't know." I stopped and turned. "Does he?"

Liam Flynn grinned up at me, halting my heart. "Get in."

Inside the car, the air-conditioning was cranked up, but that wasn't what made me shiver as I wrapped my arms around Liam's neck and kissed him like we'd been apart for a year instead of a day.

A horn honked behind us. Liam waved at the rearview mirror and put the car back into drive. "Sorry you had to take the bus again."

"I'd rather you make your PT than give me a ride home." I dug out Eric's wallet. "Besides, it was good profit."

"How much?"

I opened the wallet. "About a hundred, plus credit cards." I slipped the wallet into the compartment between the seats. "Can you make Eric's life miserable?"

"With just a few clicks of the mouse." Liam waggled his finger in the air. His hand trembled more than usual, but sometimes after physical therapy he was extra tired. "Should I give Eric the Moldavian Heiress routine or the Do-Not-Fly-List treatment?"

"Whatever you're in the mood for."

"I can't have what I'm in the mood for." He gave me a sly smile as he threaded his fingers through mine. "Not for two years."

I banged the back of my head against the headrest. "Sometimes I don't want to wait one more day. It's torture." I pulled his hand to rest on my thigh. "Now I know why most Traveller girls get married when they're fourteen."

"You're the one who wanted to wait until we finished school."

"I'll be old before I finish. After I graduate I'm going to college and then med school. And then maybe law school. Or business school, I can't decide." I stroked the back of Liam's hand. "If we got married now, I could concentrate in class instead of thinking about how much I want to see you naked."

"No, because then you'd be distracted by *memories* of me naked. Horrible flashbacks. Like nightmares, except you'd be awake."

I smacked his shoulder. "Don't even joke."

"I'm just sayin', to prepare you, for one day." He pulled his hand out of mine and smoothed the right leg of his Catholic school uniform khakis. "It ain't pretty."

"Pull over."

"Huh?"

"To the curb. Now."

He did as I asked, and I jammed the gear shift into park. Then I grabbed his thin shoulders and brought my face right up to his.

"You've always been the most beautiful boy I've ever known. You always will be. Okay?"

His gaze slid off me, like he couldn't bear the truth in my eyes. "You mean on the inside, right?"

"No!" I took his face in my hands and pressed my forehead to his. "You got any idea how late I lie awake at night, remembering every little inch of your face?" My fingertips traced his cheekbones. "I play back every kiss in my head in slow motion, again and again until I know I'll never forget it."

His sea-blue eyes searched mine, like he was looking for the teeniest chink in my faith. "Cass, I gotta tell you something."

"Go ahead."

"You gotta get out of my lap first."

I sat back in the passenger seat, knocking my knee against his cane. "Did your therapy go okay?"

"It wasn't just PT this time. I saw the doctor. It's not good."

"But you've been doing your exercises."

"I know, and if I weren't it'd be worse. But he says—" Liam hesitated, running his tongue, then his teeth, over his bottom lip before speaking to the dashboard instead of me. "He says by the time I'm twenty-one I'll probably need crutches, and when I'm twenty-five—" He swallowed. "I might be in a wheelchair."

My heart thudded at the thought, and for a second my mind blanked. But I've never been one for wallowing. "That's okay. We'll get a rancher house."

He raised his eyes to meet mine. "What?" he said, almost breathless.

"That way you won't have to worry about stairs."

"You still want to marry me?"

I hesitated. "Will you still be able to—I mean, can we still have kids?"

His face relaxed into a smile. "I'll still be able to . . . and yes, we'll have as many kids as you want. Everything still works in that department."

"Oh, good." I let out a breath I didn't even know I was holding. "Then there's nothing to worry about. My daddy gave us his blessing before he died, and not even Brendan'll break that promise." When my father drowned two years ago, his twenty-one-year-old brother married my mom. It's gross, because Brendan's young enough to be *my* brother, and now he's my stepdad. But I guess it beats her marrying some old wrinkly guy.

Traveller marriages aren't like non-Travellers' (or "country folk," as we call them when we're being nice). It's old-school—the parents make the matches, and the kids agree to it. Maybe two families want to go into business together, or a girl's father needs a son-in-law who's good at paving. Since the groom leaves his family to join his wife's, the bride's parents usually pay a dowry.

Basically, it's all about family and money and keeping our people at peace. Love is a bonus.

But I got lucky, first in having a mother who wants me to do something with my life other than get married, manage the family finances, and—most important—have lots of babies (though she says babies are 100 percent nonnegotiable).

Second lucky thing was having a father who wanted a son-in-law whose brains were bigger than his biceps. He always said we O'Rileys were special, so why should we marry someone average?

Third and most humongous lucky thing—finding Liam. Lucky, not just because he's cute and funny and kind, but because his family wasn't asking much of a dowry. Lovable *and* affordable.

"I can still drive," Liam said. "It's not like I'll be paralyzed. I just might not be able to control my legs so well all the time." He touched my face with a wobbly hand. "But I'll fight this, if I got you to fight for. I'll dance at our wedding, even if it's just a slow dance."

"You better." I snuggled up to him again, closing my eyes against the air conditioner's icy breeze. "We can practice tomorrow at Bridget's reception. I swear I'm catching that bouquet even if I have to gouge Ellie Sherlock's eyes out."

"I heard the girl who catches the bouquet at a vampire wedding has to be dessert."

I laughed. "Nuh-uh."

"It's true. I read it online."

I sat up to look him in the eyes, which sparkled all kinds of wicked. "Liar."

"Thief." He pulled me into another kiss, one without a scrap of doubt.

"Let's go to my house," I said when I could catch a breath. "Maybe Nana will be out shopping."

Liam put the car in drive so fast, the tires squealed. He watched the road as he drove, but he must've felt the way my eyes burned into him, because he didn't stop smiling.

Until he caught sight of my house.

Spooked by Liam's scowl, I flipped back the sun visor to see a man on my roof. "What does he want now?"

"What does he always want?" Liam parked in the driveway, hitting the brakes a little too hard. I handed him his cane, which he took reluctantly.

"Don't help me out of the car," he said.

"Duh." I pretended to sift through my bag for my keys, to give him time to get on his feet, so I wouldn't be waiting for him and making him look weak.

Finally I joined Liam at the end of the brick path leading to our front door. The shirtless young man on my roof, Gavin Mallory, straightened up and turned around.

"Oh, hi, Cass." He swiped the sweat off his broad, bare chest. "Hot one, huh?"

"You'll get sunburned, idiot."

"Nah, too late in the day." He cracked his knuckles, then laced his fingers behind his head, sweeping back his dark hair and displaying every muscle in his chest and arms.

To be totally honest, he was a magnificent specimen of maleness, but I'd say the same about my uncle Donal's Rottweilers, Thomas and Aquinas.

"You practicing your scams on my grandmother?" I asked him. "Pretending to fix her perfectly good roof?"

"Your dad called me, said to see if she needed any work done around the house." He finally looked at Liam. "Man's work."

"What else did Brendan say to you?" No way I'd call my stepfather by anything but his name.

"Can't tell you." Grinning, Gavin picked up the hammer and tucked a pair of nails into the corner of his mouth. "Your Nana might, if you ask real nice."

"When's he and Mama coming home?"

Gavin shrugged. "Depends."

Like most Travellers their age, my mother and stepfather went on the road during the spring to earn money. They'd get me when school let out so I could work with them, then we'd all come back here in the fall. Just because we call ourselves "Travellers" doesn't mean most of us don't have houses.

I started down the front walk and noticed Liam wasn't following me. When I turned, I saw his and Gavin's eyes locked like dogs about to fight. Or like vampires about to attack.

I rattled the screen door handle, pretending it was jammed. The noise got Liam's attention, and he followed me inside. I heard my grandmother banging around in the kitchen.

"Nana, there's a troll on the roof," I called as I sifted through the mail on the hall table. "Want me to call the exterminator?"

"Cass?" She came out of the kitchen, holding a tray of brownies in oven-mitted hands, then stopped short. "Liam."

He smiled at her. "Hi, Mrs. O'Riley. Those smell awful good."

My chest tightened as I realized the brownies had chocolate chips. Nana only made double-chocolate brownies when something bad had happened. Like when Granddad got arrested for racketeering, and later, when he was sentenced to thirty years in prison. And then again when my father died.

"Why did you make those?" I asked Nana with a quivery voice.

"I . . . uh, it's a family matter." She glanced at Liam.

I touched his arm. "Liam's family. There's nothing you can tell me that you can't tell him."

She bowed her head, then shook it slowly. That tight feeling in my chest spread to my stomach.

"It's okay. I'll go." Liam kissed my cheek. "Call you later, let you know how that thing with Eric worked out."

I'd completely forgotten about stealing my classmate's wallet. I had a feeling a school bully was about to seem like a teeny problem.

When he was gone, Nana sighed. "Such a good boy. Respects his elders. I always hoped he could teach you that." She tilted her head back toward the kitchen table. "Let's sit."

I crossed my arms. "If you have double-chocolate-brownie-worthy news, you better tell me right now."

"They're burning my fingers through these old mitts." She set them on a souvenir trivet from Bennettsville—the town where my granddad's serving out his term in federal prison—then slowly tugged off the shamrock mitts. "Your father called."

"From beyond the grave? Hallelujah, it's a miracle."

"Your stepfather," she said with an edge in her voice. "He says business is real good up there."

"Up where?"

"He can't say over the phone. Anyways, now that our family will have a little more money, he says that changes things for your future."

"Like school?" Maybe I could go to my pick of colleges instead of whichever would give me a full scholarship. Travellers don't do loans.

"No, not college." She fidgeted with her wedding ring, turning it around and around.

"Nana." I stepped forward and gently took her hands. "Tell me his exact words. That way it won't be like it came from you."

She gripped my fingers. "He said, 'Now that I've got money, I can afford a higher quality son-in-law.'" The wrinkles deepened around her eyes. "I'm so sorry, sweetpea."

I couldn't breathe in. I could only force out more and more air, like a fish stuck on a creek bank. "H . . . h . . . high . . ."

"You want to sit down?" she said. "Have a brownie?"

I drew in a breath, so hard I almost choked. "Higher quality?" I pulled away. "What am I, a mare looking for a stud? This is my life we're talking about."

"Cass—"

"And who's higher quality than Liam?"

Nana glanced at the front door. Through the screen I heard someone whistling off-tune.

I put up my hands. "Oh, no. No way. No. No. No. Not Gavin."

"Why not?"

"He's a moron."

"Well, now, not technically. His parents had him tested."

"But he doesn't know sh—he doesn't know anything about me."

"That's because you've been joined at the hip with Liam all these years. You haven't given Gavin a chance."

"Brendan can't do this. It ain't right!" I bit my lip. "It's not right. Daddy promised me to Liam."

"Like it or not, Brendan's your daddy now."

"I'm calling Mama." I slung my bag over my shoulder, then stomped into the kitchen. "After I get some brownies."

I lay on my bed, listening to my mother's voicemail greeting for the third time. After the beep, I kept going where I left off the last message:

"Liam's a master forger. And he's brilliant with online finance. Brendan thinks way too small—he doesn't get that computers are the future. All he wants to do is spray aluminum paste on people's driveways. Small, Mama, small." I poked my finger at the ceiling. "Gavin's the exact same way. Don't you want better for me? Don't you want me to be happy?" I finished in a whisper, my throat closing. "Like you were with Daddy?"

I hung up, even though there was time left on the voicemail. I stared at the ceiling, wondering what problems my country-folk classmates were obsessing over tonight. Scoring the mellowest weed? Finding the perfect flip-flops? I bet none of them was feeling their life slip away.

Footsteps clomped on the roof over my head. I wished I could put my fist through the ceiling, make the roof buckle up and knock Gavin off. Not kill him, just make him a little less "high quality."

My future husband.

No. Way.

I told my best friend, Bridget, the whole story while I helped her make centerpieces for tomorrow's reception. The theme was "Blood and Roses," probably the hundred-and-thirtieth time a vampire wedding has used it.

The bright red drops of blood on the white rose petals were fake, of course. Real blood rusts once it hits the air, because it has iron in it. I pictured my own blood rusting in my veins if I had to spend my life with Gavin Mallory.

"It's medieval," I said. "Marrying who your parents say."

"You didn't think it was medieval when you got set up with Liam." Bridget frowned at the tangled mess of baby's breath on the table. "You told him yet?"

"I'm not supposed to tell anyone until Brendan comes home and announces it officially." I leaned over to make sure Bridget's mom wasn't lurking on the basement steps. "But I'm meeting Liam tonight down by the creek. I'll tell him then, and we'll decide what to do."

"What do you mean? What's there to do?"

I shrugged and painted another streak of blood on the rose petal.

She lowered her voice. "What, Cassie, elope? You do that, you can't ever come back."

My hand trembled suddenly, almost as hard as Liam's, so I set down the rose. "We can make enough to live off of."

"It's not about money. It's about family. You'll lose everyone you ever knew."

"Including you?"

"Of course not." Her eyes turned sad. "But I don't count so much anymore."

"You count as much as ever to me." I wanted to put my arms around her, but since she'd been turned last year, she wasn't big on human hugs. She said we smelled too good.

"You didn't answer my question."

I held the rose up to the light, admiring my work. "I'd give it all up for Liam."

"Cass, you got no idea what it's like out there." Bridget started pulling the little white heads off the baby's breath.

My hand tightened, crushing the rose's soft petals. Bridget had only been fifteen when that nasty upstate vampire kidnapped her, turned her, and held her captive as his mate. Ever since my great-uncle Donal's posse killed her maker and brought her home, she never strayed far.

I reached over and scooted the rest of the baby's breath away from her, before she could rip off all the heads.

She jerked her hands back into her lap, then got up and moved to the vanity. "Must be nice, to be so sure about something. I can't even decide how to wear my hair tomorrow." She slumped onto the stool in front of the mirror. "If I was still human, I could go to the salon, but none of them are open after dark this time of year."

"I could give you a French braid." I picked up a comb so I could start dividing her long dark hair into sections.

"No." She swiped her hand over the charred-black, holy-water scar that ran from her left ear down past her collarbone. "We need to cover this as best we can." Her voice shook. "I meant, should I wear my hair curly or straight?"

"It'll be hot and humid." I kept my voice normal. "So your hair'll curl whether you tell it to or not."

"Curse of the Irish, huh?" She tugged up her blouse. "If it weren't summer I could wear a high-neck dress."

"You don't need to hide your scar. Your groom'll have one, too, remember?" My cousin Michael had been part of Uncle Donal's posse. During the raid on Bridget's maker's coven, both Michael and Bridget had gotten caught in the holy-water crossfire.

"And it'll heal one day," I reminded her. "Michael got one right after he was turned back in '93, right? Ten years later you couldn't tell it was ever there."

Her eyes went far away. "Funny. That . . . one, he said—"

Her breath hitched, and I squeezed her shoulder. She never told me much about her time in captivity, no matter how hard I tried to get her to talk. The few times she mentioned her maker, she just called him, "That . . . one."

Bridget got her voice back, all hoarse. "He said holy-water burns never heal."

"Well, that's bullshit." I lifted the veil from where it hung on the corner of her mirror. "Now put this on so we can figure out your hair. I don't know why you even care how you look. You're only marrying my sorry-ass cousin. He'll probably show up in ripped jeans and a Pearl Jam shirt."

A smile broke over her face. "Michael will look so hot in a tux."

"All vampires look hot in a tux. He's old."

"He's not even forty in human years. And he looks twenty-one."

"He still says 'rad.'"

"And in fifteen years, I'll be saying 'epic fail.' I think 'rad' will outlast that." She put a hand to her mouth. "Do people still say 'epic fail' now?"

"Sure, sometimes." My heart felt like it had been replaced by a stone. Vampires get "stuck" in the time they're turned, so they keep wearing the fashions and speaking the slang they did right before they died.

It's the same for all vampires, from what I've heard, along with flaming out in the sunlight and drinking human blood to survive. They can technically live forever, but they pick up some pretty weird habits after the first few years. I hadn't seen Bridget go crazy counting or sorting stuff yet, though Michael had certain things he had to do three times, like turn a light switch on-off-on whenever he entered a room.

But Traveller vampires have their own rules, which keeps things simple and safe for everybody:

1. No voluntary vamping—that counts as suicide for the vamped, which is a major sin. You can vamp someone to "save" their life, but it can't be the dying person's choice.

2. No drinking from country folk—secrecy equals safety, for both Travellers and vampires.

3. No drinking directly from Travellers, either. Blood gets donated, pooled, and doled out by humans (my great uncle Donal runs one of the "blood banks"). This way, the whole community supports them, plus the vampires don't know who it came from so they can't get a taste for any one person.

4. In exchange, the vampires bring in a ton of money. Their magnetism makes them master con artists, and their stealth makes them beautiful thieves. Unlike us humans, the vamps don't keep the money they earn for their own families—it gets spread out over the whole community.

5. Vampires and humans don't marry. Duh.

6. Breaking any of these rules gets you kicked out forever.

I don't know if other Irish Travellers (either here or in the Old Country) keep vampires squirreled away, but our little group has been doing it for generations. We don't talk about it when we cross paths with Travellers from Memphis or Texas or even the ones from up in Murphy Village here in South Carolina.

We don't want them stealing our secret weapon.

Down at the moonlit marsh, on a flat rock barely big enough to fit both our butts, Liam held me close while I told him how my stepfather was aiming to tear us apart and hand me over to Gavin like a piece of livestock. Through it all Liam stroked my back in big, soothing circles, not even tensing when I told him the worst parts.

When I was done, I heard nothing but the chirp of katydids. "You don't seem too surprised," I said.

"I always knew this would happen."

My heart wanted to scamper out of my chest and drown itself in the creek. "So you accept it?"

"Hell, no." He folded my left hand between his. "I always knew one day I'd have to fight to keep you. You and me were almost too good to be true."

"Almost?"

"Almost, because we are true." He brushed a curl off my cheek and tucked it behind my ear. "But still too good to be easy."

He reached into his shirt pocket and brought out two driver's licenses. I examined mine in the moonlight.

Cassandra Reynolds, age eighteen, of Little Rock, Arkansas. "Nice. And you are?"

He flipped the driver's license with a flourish, like he was dealing three-card monte. "Your devoted husband, Daniel. Age twenty-one, so I can buy us champagne for our wedding night."

"My Danny boy." I took his card and pressed it to my own, face-to-face. "Where'll we go?"

"Up north. Somewhere they can't tell a South Carolina accent from an Arkansas one."

"Somewhere they don't know about Travellers."

"That, too." He squeezed my hand, so hard I couldn't feel his own tremble. "You really wanna do this? Leave everything and everyone we know, forever?"

"It doesn't have to be forever. We go away, get married, and come back after I finish college."

"If we leave, they won't let us back. They'll say they can't trust us."

"You think if one day we show up on Mama's doorstep with her grandbaby, she'll turn us away? I'm her only child, and O'Riley women don't have many kids. So she's got lots of mothering left over."

He ran his thumb over my engagement ring. "You won't mind not having a big wedding?"

"I'd rather have a teeny tiny wedding with you than a princess's wedding to anyone else."

I raised my face to kiss him, just as my cell phone rang. I gasped at the name on the caller ID.

"Mama! Did you get my messages?"

"I got all three of them, honey." Her voice was steady and soothing, giving me hope.

"And?"

"And I understand how you feel. Believe me, I do."

My shoulders sagged with relief. "So you'll change Brendan's mind?"

She got real quiet, making me nervous.

"Mama, are you there?"

"I'm here. Look, sweetpea, you marrying Gavin is not about you and Liam. It's a lot bigger than that."

My throat closed up. She wasn't going to change Brendan's mind. She didn't even disagree.

"What's bigger?" I choked out. "What could ever be bigger?"

"Lots of things." Her voice hardened. "You've known all your life that who you marry is not about what you want. It's about doing what's right for the family, for our whole community."

"But . . ." I rubbed my lower lip to stop it from trembling. "When Daddy and Liam's father set us up, they asked us first if it was what we wanted. They wanted us to be happy." I wrapped my fingers around the edge of the stone. "And how is it good for the family and the community if I'm miserable?"

"You won't be miserable. A lot of girls would kill to marry Gavin."

"They can have him."

"You just need time to get used to the idea."

I leaned against Liam and closed my eyes as he put his arms around me. I needed his strength on top of my own to say what I was about to say.

"Mama." I spoke calmly, scrubbing the whine clear out of my voice. "I won't marry Gavin."

There was a long pause, and the next time she spoke, it was with a whisper. "I'm sorry, baby. I always wanted better for you."

She hung up. Mama was my last, best hope to help me keep my dream—me and Liam making a life here, with everyone we loved. But now, if I wanted the biggest, most important part of that dream, I'd have to steal it.

I let the phone fall on the muddy ground beside us.

"There's no choice now." Swallowing my tears, I slid my arms around Liam and held tight. "Luckily, I got an escape plan."

Vampire weddings are pretty much like human weddings, except there's no priest, no talk of kids, and instead of kissing each other, they bite.

To avoid Gavin at the reception, I stuck as close to Bridget as I could, playing the perfect maid of honor. Every time she tugged her veil to cover her burn, I got a pain in my heart, wishing for her sake the scar could have healed for the wedding. Maybe for their tenth-anniversary party.

Soon it was time for the first dance, when she and Michael left the bridal table and glided to the center of the floor, hypnotizing the whole crowd. Even the dozen or so other vampires couldn't take their eyes off the blissed-out couple as they swayed to the bittersweet sound of Martin Finnegan's band.

I headed straight for Liam, who was leaning against the far post of the open park pavilion. He was the only one watching me instead of the bride and groom—or so I thought.

He tensed suddenly, his gaze darting to my right. I veered left, but I was too late.

Gavin stepped in front of me, reeking of hair gel. "Cass, you look real pretty tonight."

"Thanks." I tugged my sky-blue wrap tighter and tried to dodge him. "So do you." Not really—if anything, he looked ridiculous, with his curls pasted down and his tie all crooked.

He put his hand on my arm to stop me. I gave him a deadly glare, which made him let go. Whatever else might be wrong with Travellers, we're not violent. Any man who beats his wife or kids will get a hundred times worse from the other men.

Gavin shoved his hands in his pockets. "Will you dance with me? Please?"

"Thank you, but I owe the first dance to my fiancé."

"Your—" He looked behind me, where I could hear the thump of Liam's cane as he approached. Then Gavin gawked at the engagement ring still on my finger. "Didn't you get the message from your dad?"

I gazed up at Gavin, my eyes wide and empty. "You mean Brendan? Nope. No message."

His jaw tightened. "You sure?"

"She said she didn't get it." Liam put his arm around me. "Is there something you want to tell us?"

Gavin's teeth ground together, and I knew he wanted to shove the news in Liam's face, but it wasn't his place to tell. Until Brendan announced it to the whole family, it might as well not be true.

Liam took my hand. "Cass, isn't this one of your favorite songs?"

"Yeah, I don't want to miss it. Bye, Gavin."

We turned for the dance floor, but Gavin grabbed Liam's shoulder. "You wait," he growled. "Your time is comin'."

"Yep. Sure is." Liam slipped out of Gavin's grip and led me away with barely a break in his stride.

"You act all smug, he'll get suspicious," I said as I looped my arms around his neck for the slow dance.

"It's hard acting normal, knowing that in an hour we'll be on that highway together." He spoke low in my ear. "Knowing that, come Monday, we'll be married, and come Monday night . . ."

My fingers tightened on his shoulders. "We have to wait until nighttime? Can't we go straight from the courthouse to our motel?"

"Whatever you want. Your whole long life, whatever you want." He gazed into my eyes. "I'll steal the stars outta the sky for you, Mary Cassidy. Every last one."

"I don't need them all. One or two might be nice, long as the sky's not using them."

I leaned my cheek against his chest as we surrendered to the music. I wondered if we'd find a place up north where a man would play Irish fiddle like Martin Finnegan.

When the song ended, Liam whispered, "My car's unlocked, next to the gazebo."

"Meet you there when they cut the cake."

We stepped away half as far as our arms would reach, but didn't let go. "I still can't believe it," he said. "I can't imagine a world where this works. It's like our life is a burning building, and I'm running down the hallway toward the door, but I can't see anything in all the smoke. I can't see you."

My stomach turned cold from the look in his eyes. "You don't dare believe it. You've always been a pessimist."

"Works for me." He winked. "That way I get a lot of good surprises."

"Keep smiling," Bridget said, clutching the knife. "It can't look like we're saying good-bye."

"I love you." I grasped her bouquet, which I'd caught even without gouging out Ellie Sherlock's eyes. "I'll miss you more than anyone."

"I love you, too. I'd give anything to hug you right now, but then everyone would know something was up. So I'll just fix your hair instead, okay?"

I swallowed the lump in my throat. "Okay."

She adjusted the tendril in front of my left ear, then touched my cheek with her soft, cool hand. "You go and love each other real good. Don't let it all be for nothing."

The crowd started to chant. "Cake. Cake. Cake. Cake! Cake!"

Bridget grinned and rolled her eyes. "Humans." Then she turned and flashed the knife. "Michael," she said in a sing-song tone. "I got something for you."

I slunk away into the applauding crowd.

My getaway bag was hidden in the bushes near the empty gazebo at the far end of the parking lot, where Liam's car sat empty. I opened the trunk, which already held his own bag.

But where was he? I stared into the patch of dark woods between the parking lot and the pavilion. Maybe the dancing had tired him out, and he was walking slower than usual.

But the prickling of my spine made me reach into the trunk for the tire iron.

In the distance, the cake music cut off, replaced by laughing and clapping. Michael must've smashed cake into Bridget's face, or vice versa. It's not like they were going to eat it—Bridget said that to a vampire, baked goods taste like sand. But their parents insisted on cake, and even vampire couples had to bow to family wishes.

When the laughter died out, I heard a thump, then another, from the woods behind me. The thumps mixed with voices and soft grunts. Then came the sound of breaking glass.

Holding the tire iron tight, I slipped my feet out of my high heels and crept into the trees, ordering myself not to whimper if I stepped on something sharp.

Way off at the pavilion, a drum rolled, and the children chanted Michael's name.

A piece of wood snapped near me, loud as a bullet.

Then came Gavin's laughter. "Liam, look what you did, boy-o. Your big fat head broke the tree."

Billy Mallory, Gavin's cousin, joined in. "What'd that tree ever do to you, gimp?"

Fear moved my feet faster, but dread kept them stealthy. My hands grew sweaty around the tire iron, and I desperately wished for a vampire's night vision.

Just before I came to the clearing, I heard a third voice say, "Shit, Gavin, I think you killed him."

I sucked in a hard gasp, then covered my mouth.

"Nah, he's still breathing," Gavin said. "Billy, what'd you do with my beer?"

Billy cackled. "I gave it to Liam, upside his head, remember?"

"Asshole. I wasn't done drinking it."

"Guys, I'm serious." The third voice, which I now recognized as Owen Mack's, shook as he spoke. "He's in real bad shape."

I reached the edge of the clearing to see the three twenty-year-olds hunched over a body that lay limp as a bag of laundry. Rage and sorrow rushed up my throat, wanting to burst out in a scream.

Gavin fished in his pocket. "Here, let's try this." He tossed something onto the ground next to Liam.

Owen picked it up. "Who's Terrell James and why do you have his YMCA card?"

"I don't have it. Liam has it, because he picked Terrell's pocket at the mall. Terrell tracked him down, beat him up, and took back his wallet. Some stuff fell out."

"So when they find Liam's body," Billy said, "they'll think Terrell did it. Good story."

"Yeah. Cops hate blacks even more than they hate Travellers."

"But what if Liam wakes up?" Owen said.

His back to me, Gavin picked up a stone twice the size of his fist and took a step toward Liam. "We'll just have to make sure he don't."

I didn't think. I flew out of the shadows and swung the tire iron at Gavin's head.

He shifted his weight in time to keep me from being a murderer myself. The iron hit his shoulder.

Gavin yelped and spun, grabbing the end of the tire iron and hurling it to the side. I didn't let go, so I swung with it, catching my foot in the hem of my dress. My forehead struck something hard. I crumpled to my knees, the world tumbling over and over.

"Cass? Oh my God, did I hurt you?" Gavin knelt by my side.

"Don't touch me!" I swung the tire iron blindly, hitting him in a soft place and making him grunt.

"Gavin, let's run," Billy shouted. "I got my car."

"Cass, I swear," Gavin said. "I didn't mean to hurt him. I just wanted to scare him into leaving you."

"Shut up and go get help." I swiped my forehead and saw blood on my fingertips. "Now!"

Owen grabbed Gavin's shoulder. "Come on!"

Gavin kept babbling. "Cass, it wasn't even my idea. It was Brendan's."

The clearing went quiet. Billy and Owen started to back away. We all stared at Gavin as his face turned plaster-pale.

"Boy, you are so dead now," Billy whispered. "If he ever finds out you told—"

"I'm sorry," Gavin said to me, lurching to his feet.

They ran. My hands curled into fists as I realized they were headed for the parking lot, not the pavilion.

"You chickenshits!" I screamed. "Get back here and help me!"

I crawled over to Liam, who lay half on his back, his legs twisted at a crooked angle. Blood ran from his mouth, nose, and ears, pooling in a puddle that soaked his golden hair.

"Liam . . ." I kissed his forehead, then forced myself to my feet. "I swear I'll be back. Don't leave me, okay? Don't you dare leave me!"

Maybe it was the dizziness, or wishful thinking, but I thought I saw his lips move. Whether it was real or not, it was all I needed.

I ran, then staggered, then crawled toward the pavilion. I tried to scream, but my weak cries were drowned out by the music.

"Cassie!"

Bridget's high-heeled pumps appeared in front of my eyes. Then her hands, holding my shoulders, giving me strength to lift my chin.

"Help . . . Liam."

"What's wrong? Where is he?"

I couldn't remember. How far had I come? It seemed like miles. "Woods." I coughed out the most important word. "Bleeding." They could follow the scent.

"We'll find him." Michael's voice was calm, in control. "Come on, Bridget."

I felt my grandmother's embrace and smelled her sharp perfume. As the darkness swallowed me whole, I prayed I'd see Liam again alive. I prayed someone would catch Gavin and make him pay.

I prayed I wasn't too late.

My ears woke before my eyes, but I couldn't make out any of the words around me. Then I realized I was surrounded by older folks whispering in Cant. They always complain that the young people can't speak it, but they use it all the time when they don't want us to understand.

I twitched my fingers and found I was lying under a fleece blanket on a thin mattress. A warm breeze blew over my face, and I heard a curtain scraping against an aluminum window frame above me. They must have carried me into an RV brought by one of the guests.

They stopped whispering, maybe because I'd moved. I tried to speak Liam's name, but my tongue was too dry.

Then, in the distance, I heard Martin Finnegan play alone. The fiddle's keening cry sliced through my mind's fog as I recognized the mournful opening notes of "Danny Boy."

My heart thudded to a halt.

They didn't play "Danny Boy" at weddings. The last time I'd heard it was at my daddy's wake.

Liam was dead.

My lips formed the word my mind was screaming, but my throat couldn't bring it to life. So it echoed around my head, louder and louder with every bounce.

NO.

"She's awake," Nana whispered in English.

I reached out for the only thing I wanted. "Liam . . ."

"Shh." She stroked my hair, pulling on the bobby pins. "You did everything you could."

I clutched the blanket, wishing my hands were wrapped around his murderers' necks. "It was Gavin and Billy and Owen."

Nana gave a deep sigh. "I thought it might be those boys. They disappeared same time as Liam. I'll tell Donal, and he'll send someone to find them."

My great-uncle would have them in his hands by the end of the weekend. Maybe even the end of the night. For killing one of their own, the three boys would probably be banished— a fate worse than death to most Travellers.

But it was a fate I'd wanted, if it meant getting to be with Liam.

I thought of his vision of our lives as a burning building. He'd never seen me standing at the door. Instead he'd fallen to the flames and smoke.

At that moment, I thought I'd fall, too, choking and burning, never to rise from the ashes. What was left in this building, anyway? A stepfather who'd wanted me to marry a murderer?

I clutched Nana's hand. "Gavin said Brendan told him to do it."

She gasped, and her fingers spasmed inside mine. "No." She shook her head so hard, I thought her dangly gold earrings would pop off.

"That's what he told me."

"Liar," she hissed.

I let go, stunned. Did she mean me or Gavin? Either way, if everyone else thought the way she did, then Brendan would never meet justice.

I turned away from her, facing the wall and tugging the blanket up tight under my chin. At that moment, I felt something I'd never felt in my entire life.

Alone.

My eyes slammed open to see the bright red numbers on my clock flash to 2:00. I remembered coming home and falling into bed, praying I'd dream of Liam's face, tonight and forever.

I was back in my room, but not alone.

"Nana?" I whispered.

"Shh." A pale figure knelt beside my bed. His blond hair glowed in the moonlight.

It was exactly the dream I'd prayed for. *Thank you, God, for small kindnesses.* I opened my mouth to speak Liam's name.

But quick as a magician, he placed his finger against my lips. "Don't speak. Don't move. Everything depends on it."

Confusion paralyzed my muscles. I didn't understand why instinct told me to obey him without question.

Then I realized why. This was no dream.

And Liam's hand no longer trembled.

"It's me," he said in the softest whisper. "It's still me."

My breath quickened, and a shiver worked its way up my spine until my shoulders shook. A tear slipped out of my left eye, dripping over the bridge of my nose. Bridget had saved him the only way she could.

He wiped my tear away. "Fear not, Mary Cassidy."

In an instant, my sorrow flipped to joy. Alive or undead, it *was* still Liam.

I narrowed my eyes. "I may be a virgin Mary, but you sure as heck ain't no angel Gabriel."

"I told you to shhh." He pressed his finger to my lips again.

I kissed it, holding his gaze. "Make me shhh."

His eyelids went heavy, and he leaned in, so slowly I moaned.

He stopped. "You know what I am now?"

"You're in this world. That's all that counts."

His eyes opened wide, then crinkled at the edges. "I was wrong, Cass. We are too good to be true."

"Luckily we don't give two shits about the truth." I placed my hand over his heart, which beat as strong as when he was alive. Then I looped my fingers into his shirt collar, giving it a tug. "Kiss me."

"It could be dangerous."

"Good."

"Not we-might-get-arrested dangerous. More like, I-might-chomp-your-tongue-off dangerous. If I get thirsty."

I touched his cheek. "You're warm. You're not thirsty."

"I drank before I came here. But I'm so young, I could be starving any second."

"Then either kiss me or go away. I hate when you tease."

He leaned in close again. "Liar."

"Thief."

He brushed his lips against mine, soft as a wish.

"Get away from her," growled a commanding voice, "before I tear your damn fool head off."

Liam put his hands up and slowly leaned away from me, revealing my cousin Michael silhouetted in the doorway. The light flashed on, then off, then on again.

"Are you psycho?" Michael yanked Liam to his feet. "You want to get staked your first night undead?"

"I had to see her."

"And now you have." He dragged Liam toward the door. "For the last time."

I sat up. "Where are you taking him?"

"Away from humans."

I leaped out of bed and followed them into the hallway. "Wait!"

Michael stopped short, and they turned to me. Liam's gaze dropped to my thighs. I realized how short my sleep shirt was.

I put my hands on my hips, hiking the shirt higher. "He's still my fiancé."

Michael's eyes went cold, his scowl made fiercer by the jagged black scar across his right cheek and the bridge of his nose.

"You can't marry a vampire." His voice was flat and patronizing, like he'd said, "You can't milk a frog."

"Michael's right." Nana's voice came from behind me. I turned to see her in her flannel nightgown. "Liam can't grow old with you. He can't even go outside during the day." She raised her palms. "Most of all, he can't give you children."

Reality slammed me, almost knocking me off my feet.

Liam and I stared at each other. His life on earth had just been doubled, but his future with me had been cut to nothing.

Yet I loved him not one tiny bit less, and needed our Now more than ever.

"Fine," I said. "I won't get married."

My grandmother's face darkened like a storm cloud. "Go to your room. Michael—take that boy home."

"You got it, Aunt Kate." Before I could take a step toward Liam, my cousin had dragged him down the stairs toward the front door.

I ran to my bedroom window and pushed aside the curtain.

Nana entered behind me. "Don't you ever say a thing like that. Not get married. You want to give your grandmother a heart attack?"

Michael and Liam crossed the lawn. Even as he walked sideways to keep my window in sight, Liam's steps were sure and straight, the way they'd never been in life.

"Plenty of women stay single," I told her.

"Oh my." She sank onto my bed, like she was feeling faint. "I told your mama not to send you to public school. I knew it'd put crazy ideas into that head of yours."

"My head is fine." I rubbed my temple, then dropped my hand quickly before she started up again, worrying I had a concussion.

"Being single is fine for those depraved country folk, but not for Travellers. Don't you even care what you are?"

"What I am is in love with Liam, and sick of this life. I'm going to college. How can I do that with babies running all around?"

"Your mama will help you take care of them. And your husband, whoever he ends up being."

"You mean whoever Brendan sets me up with. What if my husband doesn't want me to go to college? Or what if he wants me to run cons with him when I should be studying? Most people can't live that double life—they want it one way or the other, inside or out. But Liam and I could've done it." I watched Michael shove him into the front seat of the car. "Maybe we still can."

"Mary Cassidy O'Riley." For once, my grandmother spoke my full name gently. "Whatever you decide, I will always love you."

My eyes blurred with tears.

"But if you leave us, I'll mourn you. I'll mourn like you were six feet under ground." She went to the door. "We all will."

I watched Michael drive away, with Liam's pale face turned my way until they were out of sight. Then I slouched back over to the bed, wanting to do nothing but lie down and cry the rest of the night away.

My throat still parched, I reached for the water I'd left on my nightstand, then gasped.

Next to the glass sat Bridget's bridal bouquet, the one I'd caught. I picked it up and took a deep whiff of the red and white roses, wondering how it had gotten here. I'd left it in Liam's car along with my getaway bag earlier that night. Before he died.

He'd brought it back to me.

I looked at the clock, calculated the hours until sunrise (three), then hurried to my desk. While my laptop started up, I changed my clothes and filled my backpack with everything I truly needed. I was used to living out of an RV for an entire summer, so I knew how to pack light. Besides, I had something else to pick up.

Downstairs, I left a note on the kitchen counter:

> Dear Nana,
>
> I hope one day, you'll let me live again.
>
> Love, Mary Cassidy O'Riley

Michael blocked the doorway of his bungalow, which was now Bridget's and Liam's home, too. He'd changed out of his tuxedo, back into his usual flannel shirt and jeans.

"I told you, Cass, you can't see him."

"I'm not here to see Liam. I'm here to see you."

He glanced toward the side of the house, like he expected someone to jump out with a crossbow, then at the heavy plastic cooler in my hand. "Is this a trick?"

I smiled up at him. "Me? Tricky?"

My cousin nodded grimly and started to shut the door, but I put my foot across the threshold.

"Michael, I'm kidding. Let me in and I'll explain."

He gave a heavy sigh and called over his shoulder. "Bridget, take the kid into the den." In response to a voice I couldn't hear, he said, "So he doesn't eat his ex-girlfriend, that's why. And stay with him."

I followed him into the kitchen. "You need to learn to say please. Didn't you read the husband book?"

He scratched his head as he pulled a beer out of the fridge. "There's a book?"

I set the cooler on top of the counter with a thud, then flipped back the lid.

"What's that?" Michael stepped closer, wary as a fox sniffing bait in a trap. His eyes widened when he saw what was inside. "Shit, Cassie. Where'd you get all that blood?"

"Where do you think?"

"You broke into my dad's blood bank?" His fingers twitched on the beer bottle, rubbing the edge of the label. "How'd you get past the dogs?"

"He took them with him to hunt down Gavin and his boys. The lock was easy. And he won't know it's gone until at least tomorrow."

"Yeah, and then we'll all catch holy hell." Michael reached into the cooler and pulled out a smooth plastic bag of blood. "It's a great wedding gift, but you gotta take it back."

"It's not a wedding gift." My eyes shifted toward the den.

"Cass, I told you to let Liam go. You're not safe around him, and the sooner you move on, the better off we'll all be." Michael plopped the bag back in the cooler. "Bridget and I'll take care of him. He's fine."

"Don't lie to her." Bridget entered the kitchen, her stomps rattling the glasses in the cupboard even though she was perfectly capable of stealth. "The boy's on a goddamn hunger strike."

"A hunger strike?" My blood felt as cold as the blood in the cooler. "Why?"

"It won't last," Michael said.

"He says he won't drink until we let you be together." Bridget peered into the cooler. "Oh my Lord, are you out of your mind?" She backed up out of reach and put her hands behind her. "Get that out of our house. If they catch us with that much blood at one time—that'd last all three of us for a week, maybe longer."

I closed the lid slowly, snapping it shut. "I know it would."

She squinted at me. "What are you saying?"

"I'm saying I'm getting me and Liam out of here, and I need your help."

"What did I just tell you?" Michael slammed the bottom of his bottle on the counter, so hard it fizzed up and over-flowed. "You can't be with him."

"Calm down." Bridget pointed at him like he was a mis-behaving puppy. "Let me handle this."

He pressed his lips together, then backed off and wiped the wet bottle on his shirttail, glaring at us but staying quiet. Maybe he did read the husband book.

She turned back to me. "It was bad enough you running off yesterday when Liam was alive. I didn't agree with it, but I went along anyway because you're my friend and I want you to be happy. But now—"

"Now we need to leave more than ever. You just said Liam's on a hunger strike. You're his maker—you can't let him die."

"We're both his makers." She gazed sadly at Michael. "I tried to do it all by my myself, but I guess I'm too young a vampire."

He said nothing, just stared at the floor.

"Michael, I didn't know," I whispered. "Thank you."

"I knew how sad you'd be if Liam died." He smirked. "And that you'd go off and kill those boys yourself, so I figured I was saving more than one life."

"So what did you save him for, if not to be with me?"

He scratched the side of his head and didn't answer.

"Cass," Bridget said. "It's not so simple running away when you're a vampire. The sun'll kill us."

"I thought of that. If we leave by four-thirty, we can make it to a vampire-safe motel before sunrise. I already got us a room."

She blinked at me. "A vampire-safe motel?"

I nodded to the stapled stack of papers I'd left on the counter. "I looked it up before I left. There's 'vampire-friendly' places, which means they're either run by vamps or humans who know what you are. Then there's 'vampire-safe,' which just means they have rooms without windows, or at least a bathroom you can sleep in during the day."

She picked up the papers and flipped through them, her eyes turning wide with wonder. "So there are other vampires out there who live around humans, like we do? Vampires who aren't like that . . . one?"

"There must be." I stepped closer to her. "I know it's asking a lot. You have a life here, and you're scared to leave. But if you help me, I'll help you. I can get whatever you need during the day. You don't have to be scared."

Bridget chewed her thumbnail as she slowly set down the papers, then stared at the door to the den for a long moment. Finally she looked at the clock. "So we got forty-five minutes."

"What?" Michael shouldered his way between us. "Bridget, we're not doing this."

"Maybe *we* aren't." She reached past him and took my hand. "But I am."

Though her hand was cool, my whole body turned warm. I vowed to myself that she'd never regret this. Even if, every once in a while, it meant opening my own veins.

Michael stepped back, almost staggering. "Bridget, you . . . you want to leave me? On our wedding night?"

"No, I don't want to!" Her voice choked with tears. "But they need my help. Cass and Liam were there for me after I was turned."

"So was I!"

"And I love you for it, and for a million other reasons. But Liam could die. You'll survive without me."

"I don't know about that." He raised his arms to the walls, like the house was already empty without her. "What about the family?"

"I'm your family, too," I reminded him. "You loved me enough to save Liam once."

He shut his eyes hard. I held my breath, waiting for his decision. We didn't need Michael to help us escape, but God only knew what they'd do to him if they thought he didn't try hard enough to stop us. And Bridget would be miserable without him.

Then he shook his head. "We can't take Cass away," he told Bridget. "That's kidnapping. They'll hunt us down and kill us. Just like we did to your maker."

"No, they won't." Liam appeared in the doorway, his face and eyes paler than ever. "Not if we're already dead."

They let me light the fuse.

It was the safest bet, since one touch of flame wouldn't make me poof into nothingness. Besides, out of all of us, I had the most to lose from leaving this place. And the most to gain.

We parked on the far side of the marsh to watch Michael's house burn. Michael and I sat on the hood, with Bridget and Liam on the trunk. Like it was Fourth of July and the Kiwanis Club was setting off fireworks down at the park.

The trunk of Bridget's car held the cooler of blood, along with a pair of shotguns, three blackout curtains, and about eight grand in cash. Anything else we needed, we could buy, beg, or steal. Probably steal.

As the flames shot into the sky and sirens began to wail, Liam came to stand next to me.

"Remember when the bunch of us built that treehouse in Michael's backyard?" he said. "We said one day we'd live in it together."

"Yeah. Except the floor kept falling through when Gavin pulled out the nails." I bit my lip, wishing I hadn't said that name.

"I'll find him one day," he said, steady as the wind. "And I'll be more careful with him than he was with me." His pupils dilated suddenly, reflecting the distant flames. "Careful the blood runs slow while I'm taking him apart. Careful he stays awake till the very end."

The chill in his voice stopped my heart. I wanted to kill Gavin myself then, for turning my sweet, tender boy into a monster.

A monster I refused to fear.

"How do you feel?" I asked Liam. "Besides, you know . . ."

"Bitter? Desperate? Furious?" He drew his left hand down his right arm. "I feel perfect."

I took Liam's hand, wondering when I would stop expecting it to tremble.

Bridget hopped off the trunk and jingled her keys. "Let's roll before we get fried."

We got in the car, Michael and me in back and Liam up front with Bridget in case he got hungry and I started looking tastier than the blood bags in the cooler. She set the GPS for the vampire-safe motel in Summerville.

The road took us north a few miles and up a hill, so I could watch the black sky turn purple as dawn spread over the ocean. My heart twisted as I realized Liam was an hour away from his first missed sunrise.

We'd find our way back to each other, not as what we used to be—two Traveller kids destined to share a life—but as what we were now, a vampire and a . . . whatever I was. We'd mourn his life, for a long time. We'd mourn the lives we'd never create, forever.

Deep down I knew I was leaving home for myself as much as I was leaving for Liam. I needed my own life, even if I had to steal it.

We crossed the bridge and headed inland, putting the sun and sea behind us. I turned forward then, ready to face whatever lay ahead.

At least we were on the road, where anything's possible.

About the Authors

Claudia Gray is the Chicago-based author of the *New York Times* bestselling Evernight series, set in the present day, in which Patrice is a character—now as a 160-year-old vampire. You can learn more about her work at www.claudiagray.com.

Lili St. Crow is the author of the Strange Angels series and, as Lilith Saintcrow, the author of the Dante Valentine and Jill Kismet series. She lives in Vancouver, Washington, with her children, a houseful of cats, and assorted other strays. Visit her online at www.lilithsaintcrow.com.

Nancy Holder is the *New York Times* bestselling coauthor (with Debbie Viguié) of the young adult dark fantasy series Wicked, which has been optioned by DreamWorks. She and Viguié have sold two more young adult dark fantasy series: Crusade, their vampire trilogy, debuted in September 2010; The Wolf Spring Chronicles will come out in December 2011. She has sold eighty novels, and written novels, short fiction, and episode guides for *Buffy the Vampire Slayer, Angel, Smallville*, and many other shows. She is the winner of four Bram Stoker awards. She lives in San Diego, with her daughter and coauthor, Belle.

Heather Brewer was not your typical teen growing up and she's certainly not your typical adult now. When she's not writing about vampires, she's contemplating world domination. She carries a stuffed gargoyle, believes in the presence of ghosts, and is relatively certain that Gerard Way is actually a creature of the night. Heather is the author of the *New York Times* bestselling series The Chronicles of Vladimir Todd. She doesn't believe in happy endings . . . unless they involve blood. She lives in Missouri with her husband and two children. Visit Heather at www.heatherbrewer.com.

Rachel Caine is the author of the internationally bestselling Morganville Vampires series, as well as the Weather Warden and Outcast Season series. She grew up in the wilds of West Texas, and swears that Morganville probably exists somewhere out there in all that unknown open country. She currently lives in Fort Worth, Texas, with her husband, noted artist R. Cat Conrad, and their two iguanas, Popeye and Darwin.

Award-winning author **Jeri Smith-Ready** lives in Maryland with her husband, two cats, and the world's goofiest greyhound. Her novels include the Shade ghost series for teens and the WVMP Radio adult vampire series, the cast of which Cass and Liam will soon join. When not writing, Jeri can usually be found—well, thinking about writing, or on Twitter. Like her characters, she loves music, movies, and staying up very, very late. Visit her at www.jerismithready.com.

Nyx in the House of Night

Edited by P.C. Cast

Delve into the real mythology,
folklore, and religion behind
P.C. and Kristin Cast's
House of Night series with
P.C. Cast as your guide

Wiccan ritual * the island of Skye
Nyx and Erebus * Cherokee legend * and more